Holiday Hoopla

Dana Volney

CRIMSON
ROMANCE

F+W Media, Inc.

This edition published by
Crimson Romance
an imprint of F+W Media, Inc.
10151 Carver Road, Suite 200
Blue Ash, Ohio 45242
www.crimsonromance.com

ISBN 10: 1-4405-7499-5
ISBN 13: 978-1-4405-7499-3
eISBN 10: 1-4405-7500-2
eISBN 13: 978-1-4405-7500-6

Cover art © iStock.com/monkeybusinessimages

To Dad, Mom, Marissa, and Chris—for endlessly supporting my whimsy and only interjecting reality twenty-six percent of the time. I truly love you.

Acknowledgments

First and foremost I am grateful to the entire Crimson Romance team for being so marvelous to work with, and for taking a chance on a first time author. A special thank you to Tara Gelsomino and Julie Sturgeon for being delightful and amazing! Julie, you definitely made the sea of blue bearable, are the champion of all night owls, and I sincerely hope we get to work together again.

Mary Billiter—thank you for being a sounding board, cheerleader, empathizer, competitor, mentor, and friend. And, soon to be conference buddy! Someday I will find the Hawaiian punch scent, you just wait. You have made this entire experience one of a kind (in a good way). You are a treasure.

Neva Bodin and Nurieh Glasgow—thank you for your time, insight, and camaraderie!

A big shout out to my Wednesday night writing class peeps—you rock and your fellowship lifts me every week!

Thank you to friends and family who have, and continue to, support my dreams. You inspire me every day and are appreciated!

Chapter One

Halle Adams leaned against the counter and propped herself up on her elbows. She stared at the pink bottle brush Christmas tree on the jewelry case. The glittered star shimmered in the Christmas lights. *So simple. So pretty. So ...* She sighed. Earlier, when she'd poured herself a glass of wine, she'd cut the overhead lights and opted for the glow from the store's Christmas tree. She loved and hated this time of year. The beauty of the holiday was undeniable ... the Christmas lights, decorations, even the music that piped out of her storefront speakers onto First Street. Passersby in her town of Casper, Wyoming caught a bit of the holiday cheer when they strolled past her newly decorated window displays full of short evergreen trees with hanging candy canes, wooden reindeers wearing her necklaces, and scarves and hats and rustic plaques proclaiming holiday cheer. On her door hung a bedazzled "open" sign. Twinkling lights cast a blinking reflection of her store marquee, Just Dandy, on the snow-dusted sidewalk. *Just Dandy. Just Dandy. Just Dandy ... Yeah, like that was going to happen any time soon after this muck up.*

The Christmas season had been magical since she was a little girl, but these days it also stirred up a restlessness she was only able to tame the rest of the year. Halle twisted the stem of the hand painted wine glass between her fingers. The end of a year, particularly after Thanksgiving, brought an emptiness with it that usually inspired her to act on a reckless whim. *Not that thinking things out works well. Case in point—Dad. I've got to break free from his strings.* She had a little over a month to really make this year count. There was something more to this life, something she knew she should do … she just hadn't been able to put a finger on it. Maybe if she hired Christmas carolers to serenade her customers the joy would rub off on her. People were happy everywhere, and while she mostly related, something was missing.

The front door's jingle startled her.

"Hello?" A gruff voice called out. "Are ya open?"

She raised her voice toward the front door, "Yeah, back here."

Halle quickly stood, forgetting she held a glass of wine. The blush liquid sloshed over the side and onto her hand.

"Shoot." She checked the sleeve of her white V-neck. *Whew. Close one.* She looked up and caught a penetrating stare from the man who'd just entered her store.

"Hazards of drinking on the job?" A slow grin spread across his stubbled face.

"Quality control." She shrugged, adding a wink and a coy smile. "Someone's gotta check the merchandise."

Halle's gaze wandered over the stranger in the dim Christmas tree lighting. His broad build filled out his tan North Face jacket. She didn't have to look down to know he was in jeans and cowboy boots. *Why, hello. Merry Christmas to me.* Halle set down her wine glass and felt heat start at her toes and rise to her throat. She wasn't sure if the sensation moving through her was the wine or her body talking.

"What are you in need of today?" She reached for a rag beneath the counter and hastily wiped her hand before resting her gaze back on the cowboy. His deep, brown eyes matched his wavy, brown hair. Thick eyelashes intensified his dreamy stare. *Those are eyes I bet no woman gets tired of.* Halle mused at the giddiness that tingled her midsection.

"I need to find a present for my sister. I know she likes this place. Are you sure you're open?" He looked at the ceiling. "Are your lights working?"

"They are now, but . . ." She shook her head before laughing in attempt to deflect the situation. "Check back next week."

The man's brows rose in a query.

Halle moved around the counter and flipped on the light switch by the front door. "Seemed like a twinkle light kinda afternoon." She straightened her sweater against her jeans. She couldn't seem to stop grinning. *Don't act like you're in high school, Halle. This guy's a customer. Even if he does smell good. Like the forest.* She'd never been a fan of evergreen, but this cowboy made it heavenly.

"So, you need a gift for your sister?"

He turned and looked around the store. Halle took the opportunity to check him out. *About my age . . . no ring. Why haven't I ever met him before? This town isn't that big.* Halle bit the side of her bottom lip. Her "consequences-be-damned-there-is-fun-to-be-had" streak was pulsing through her body, and this cowboy made her feel like being naughty. *Here I thought the holiday season was going to be boring.*

The stranger peered over the rack of spices and miscellaneous cooking items. "I didn't realize you had a bunch of different stuff in here."

"Sure do—something for everyone. What does she like?"

"Blue." He looked up. "She loves blue."

"Blue . . . okay. I have some blue necklaces I made over here." She motioned to the glass cases that doubled as her front counter. "I also have a matching scarf and hat set in ocean blue." She scooped up the items and held them toward him.

"Oh, those are nice. You make this stuff?"

"Some of it—mostly the necklaces." She caught his gaze and lowered her voice in mischief. "Sometimes, when I'm feeling really sexy, I crochet."

"That's weird. So do I." His lips started to curve up until the chirping sound of his cell phone suddenly cut it short. He retrieved it from his front jean pocket.

"Excuse me." He turned his back to her and spoke quietly into the phone. All she could hear was mumbling.

Halle laid the crocheted set on the counter and spied her wine glass. *Where does drinking during a transaction stand on the appropriate meter? Hell, I own the joint.* The words of her father sounded off in her head causing an eye roll. She owned the business, not the physical store, as he'd so astutely pointed out in what had started as a civilized meeting last week.

She moved to retrieve her glass when she heard a low "sonuva—"

"What?" Halle stopped in her tracks just out of reach of her glass.

She wracked her brain for what the problem could be. Maybe she'd had one too many glasses of wine. No, wait; she did a mental count. She'd only been on glass number two when whoever this was walked in and made her spill half of her new glass.

"No. Not you." He pocketed his phone and looked at her. "Family issues."

"Family, huh? They'll getcha." *Yeah, that was clearly the best thing to say. Oh well, he's nice to look at.* She let her gaze wander down his nicely fitted jeans to his cowboy boots, and back up. After all, it was the holidays; everyone deserved a little happiness, right? Even her.

•••

Blake Ellison continued to watch the woman. *Can't I have a moment of peace? I can't even Christmas shop without ... This gal has the right idea, drinking in the afternoon. That's my kind of day.* He wished it was just because of the holidays, but lately his life was complicated with unfair obligations that made him want to drink—a lot … a whole lot.

Blake assessed the friendly sales gal. Her blonde hair was tied back in a messy ponytail that was weirdly sensual. Her fresh face was a welcome relief from the overly made up women he usually encountered.

"I'm Blake by the way." He offered his hand.

"Halle, nice to meet you." She slipped her hand in his firmly. *Strong. Good.* Limp fish handshakes were the worst.

"You don't happen to have another glass or bottle of beer hiding back there, do ya?" He raised an eyebrow again.

Halle laughed and her green eyes danced. He grinned, getting swept up in the moment.

"Tsk, tsk." She crinkled her nose. "Isn't it a little early?"

"Well, you made it look so fun." He cocked his head toward the counter where she'd spilled what smelled like a Zinfandel.

"You, my new friend, are in luck. I happen to have a glass and, better yet, a new bottle."

She knelt down to fish under the counter and Blake leaned over to check out the view his higher perch now afforded him. *Sexy.* Halle popped back up and his startled eyes found hers. She fetched a decorated glass off the shelf and waggled it in her hand.

"Convenient." He nodded toward the spot she'd just made vacant.

"Perk of being the owner." She winked and headed to the back of her store.

Blake wasn't sure what do to, but he followed because she had wine. *She owns this place? Huh.* He couldn't keep his eyes from roaming. *Nice ass.*

Halle motioned to a couple of high backed, brightly patterned green and pink chairs. A sitting area had been set up in the middle of the store, complete with an end table between the chairs and a rug. They sat and she poured.

"Cheers."

They clinked glasses.

"So, Blake, what drives you to drink in the middle of the day?" Halle crossed her legs and shifted to look at him.

Too long to explain, Halle. He took a long swig and swirled the remaining liquid. Where did he start to explain his grandpa's recent death, and how his dad was using it to railroad him to stay in the banking business to someone he'd known for all of five minutes. Or should he start with how he wanted to run his family's ranch and not let his dad sell it? Better yet, he could lead with all the questions about his dating life that increased around Christmas and the set ups that inevitably followed. It was the worst time of year to be single.

"Does there have to be a reason?" he asked.

"Nope. But, then I think that crosses the line from fun to you have a problem."

He didn't look, but he knew she was smiling as she razzed him.

"My reason ... hmm ... pressure." He thought about another pull but decided to pace himself. *I wish this was beer.*

He surveyed the store to continue avoiding her, pretending interest in the candle display, the clothes, the Western knickknacks, and the contemporary furniture. Blake's defenses were down and he didn't feel like building a mental wall right now. He just wanted to sit in the middle of the small, eclectic shop and drink. *There's probably something wrong with this, but ... eh, I don't care.*

"Wow. No wonder you need a drink. Those *pressures.*"

He watched as she playfully rolled her eyes in sarcasm. She was pretty—not the strikingly beautiful kind, but the solidly attractive type; the type that made him want to reach out and fold her into his arms. She looked soft and touchable. He could use a hug. *Man, one call from Sis and I'm needing a hug. Shit.* He drank.

"Okay then, why were *you* drinking?" He didn't want to talk about himself. Learning more about Halle was more pleasing.

"This normal for you? I'm sure we can get you into a good twelve-step program."

"I was *thinking*." She bobbed her head his way.

"In the dark with wine?"

"Surrounded by Christmas lights," she raised her finger and circled it in the air, "*not* in the dark." Halle drank. She let out a sigh before she continued. "Truth be told, I was denied something I need. And, I'm not in love with the options I'm left to consider."

"Denied? Right." He jeered. *Who would deny her?*

"Yeah. I need a business loan and the bank said no."

"Oh for a *loan*." *Pay attention, man.*

She scoffed, "What did you think I meant?"

"Um, nothing." He cleared his throat. "So this bank. Which one?"

"North Platte River Bank."

What? Blake shifted in his seat, squaring up with her the best he could in a chair that was not made for a tall man. *Good thing I didn't tell her my last name.*

"I see," was all he managed to reply.

His mind started buzzing as a thought crossed it. What he needed to survive the holidays was to buy some time to figure out a way to keep the ranch in the family—and a distraction. Questions about Halle would preempt any about business. Halle wouldn't look bad on his arm ... maybe.

"What was the loan for?" he asked.

Halle fidgeted and peered at him over her wine glass. "I want to buy my own building. This place is great, off Main Street and everything, but the rent is *killing* me. I'd like to be independent. I thought I had it all figured out . . ." Her voice trailed off and so did her gaze.

"You don't think a new location would hurt business?"

"Nope." She shook her head. "I started Just Dandy five years ago. I have a following." She leaned her head back. "I have a newsletter, website, and who wouldn't want to attend a moving party, then a grand opening party?" She took another swig. "Party." She raised her glass in the air.

Blake laughed and shook his head. He understood. Give people food and booze and they were happy. *She's business minded and cute. My family would totally eat this up. But, will she go for it?*

"Maybe we could help each other out." He finished his wine, set the glass down on the end table, and leaned forward.

"What?"

"My pressures?" Blake turned his head toward her, finding her still leaned back in her chair. "Well, for starters, I need a date to accompany me to all of these bloody holiday gatherings, family parties, and other political nonsense I'm required to attend."

"Okay." She squinted at him. "And I get . . ."

He shrugged his shoulders. "A loan."

"What?" Her face lit up.

Blake searched her eyes. Over the years he'd learned to listen to his instincts. His stomach didn't drop or twist, which was always the sign of something bad—no, instead he felt something else. Intrigue? Happiness, maybe?

"I can make sure you get a business loan. Whatever amount you need."

Blake internally cringed at the part of this conversation that was inevitable. He hated telling people his last name and watching them put it all together, always treating him differently afterward, making it hard to tell who his real friends were.

• • •

Halle sat straight up. *Who the hell is he?* She quickly did a mental recap but was still coming up blank as to who this Blake fellow was. She didn't recognize him from anywhere. She'd grown up in Casper but moved in her late teens when the relationship between her parents had deteriorated. Living with her mom had been a hard decision, being the only child, but it had been the right one. After college she had decided to move back to Casper to start fresh with her dad. That only lasted for a couple of years. Right up until he wanted to wipe out a protected wildlife habitat for a new mall. That was the line in the sand for both of them.

"How could *you* get me a loan?" She heard the sarcasm in her voice but didn't care.

He was still looking at her, hard. It was starting to make her uncomfortable in a hot and bothered kind of way.

He broke contact, stared at his cowboy boots, rubbing the back of his neck. "Trust me, I can make it happen."

"Yeah, okay, cowboy. I'll just *trust you*." Halle finished off her glass of wine. *I'm drinking with a crazy person. Go figure.* She stood and started for the front of the store so he'd get the hint it was time for him to leave.

She heard a long sigh behind her.

"I'm Blake Ellison."

She froze between the rhinestone purses and flashy belts. *Ellison.* She whirled around and faced him. Blake sat back in his chair, folding one long leg over the other, ankle to knee.

"*You're* an Ellison?" She furrowed her brows at him. "And *you* can't find a date?"

"No, I can find a date. That's not what I want, though." He reached for the wine bottle and filled both glasses to the top.

"I'm confused. Didn't you say you needed a date?"

"Yep." Blake scratched the back of his head, rumpling his brown hair. "But, not a date that's trying to impress anyone." The sides of his laughing eyes crinkled. "I want a *real* person. I want a real date."

Gorgeous with perfect teeth. Adrenaline mixed with nerves danced around her head and then her heart and finally settled in her stomach. *There has to be a catch.*

Blake continued, "You seem fun. And, I would know why you're there … no need to second guess your motivation."

She didn't remember walking back to her chair and sitting, but suddenly she was picking up her glass of wine. She appreciated his logic. "So you'd like me, a total stranger, to go with you to your functions? I could be bat crazy for all you know."

"Nah, I'm a good judge of character." He shook his head and took a drink while eyeing her.

"And for going to a couple of events, you'll make sure my loan goes through?"

"Yup."

Halle eyed him. "You have the power to do that? You're not like a second cousin twice removed or anything like that?"

"Nope. Grandson of the founder of the family businesses. Direct line."

How bad could it hurt? The food was always great at these things.

"Alright." She waved a hand toward him and let it fall hard on her thigh. "I'm in." What the heck? She'd done more impulsive things in her life.

"Perfect." He retrieved his phone. "Let's look at the calendar and sync our schedules, shall we?"

It was time to stop letting her father call the shots. Now she was going to have the means to do that. Even if she had to go to events she swore off long ago, it was a small price to pay for independence. *Will Dad be there?* Her heart stopped until she remembered him mentioning that he and his new wife, Leigh, would be gallivanting across Europe for most of December. She stifled a laugh. It would be almost hilarious to run into him at one of these events and be on Blake's arm. She'd probably witness her dad speechless for the first time in his life.

Her schedule was pitifully empty and she marked every date and time down in her phone calendar. She took care to hide her screen so Blake wouldn't know just how not in demand she was these days. The first of several events, a banquet for the employees of Ellison-owned businesses, was Friday, just two days away. "How formal is it?" Halle wondered out loud, tapping her finger on her chin. *Either way, I'm gonna need some new dresses.*

"Pretty formal." Blake eyed her up and down. "You got something to wear?"

"Sure. No problem."

"So, we're agreed, classy?"

"Sir." She fanned herself, batting her eyelashes. "Your insults abound."

Blake laughed and Halle shook her head. *Of course I'll keep it classy. Who does he usually take to these things?* Halle knew Corrine, her best friend and owner of the dress shop next door, would have just what she needed.

• • •

The next day, Halle bounced over to Dress to Impress where she found Corrine in the back with a needle, thread, and pieces of yellow fabric.

"How's it going?" Halle asked.

"Just fightin' with life." Corrine's head was down. "Good thing my mama taught me how to sew."

Halle chuckled as she watched her friend. Streaks of pink contrasted starkly against Corrine's black locks. "Nice hair."

Corrine's head shot up. "You like it? Just got it done last night. The girls at bingo are gonna flip." She used her free hand to pat her new do. "I love it."

Halle wasn't as brave as Corrine even though Halle was twenty years younger. *Bravery must come with age.* Her own hair had been blonde with blonde highlights for as long as she could remember.

Refocusing on the reason for her visit, Halle headed toward the racks of dresses. "I need a couple of dresses for stuff this month. Can you help me find something?"

"Sure, doll. Have some fancy parties to go to?"

"Well, actually, yes."

"What?" Corrine's voice was more surprised than Halle thought it should've been. "With who? What did I miss?"

"Oh, it's no big deal." Halle diverted her eyes on purpose. It wasn't a big deal and she didn't want Corrine thinking it was. "Just an ... old friend who needs a date to some holiday events."

"Hmm. I thought you'd sworn off all that jazz?" Corrine studied her for a beat.

Halle's eyes widened and she pressed her lips together. Corrine had always been able to figure her out. Halle's best defense was silence.

"You'll tell me," Corrine's voice was slow and matter of fact. "You always do."

"That's all there is to it. I need a formal dress for a banquet this Friday. Any ideas?"

"You certainly can't go in this." Corrine wagged her hand up and down in a zigzag motion.

"Yoga pants won't cut it? My birth control glasses are a deterrent of some sort?" Halle rolled her eyes. "Geez." She was thankful that yesterday she'd gone with contacts—just like she would for all of December now.

"I just wanted to be sure." Corrine raised her hands up, palms out. "I know it's been a while since Justin."

"It hasn't been *that* long and I know how to act on a date ... um, friend thing."

"He was," Corrine looked to the ceiling, "six months ago. You need to get back out there."

"I'm out there," Halle said weakly.

"Um, no. You're not."

"How do you figure? I went out with that guy, Corbin, just the other day."

"First of all, that was at least a month ago. Second, it was a drink. That doesn't count as a date. Third, he asked you out again and you declined when there was nothing wrong with him."

She'd declined a *real* date because not only did she know Corbin's life's story but also his ex-girlfriend's. She couldn't sit through drinks or otherwise again and listen to him speak about someone he was clearly not over.

"Eh, so dating isn't my thing right now." She peered at Corrine from the racks. "We all aren't as lucky as you. High school sweethearts aren't as easy to find these days."

"Maybe. But that doesn't mean you give up."

"I'm not giving up. I'm just taking a hiatus."

"Call it what you will. I'm this close," Corrine held her thumb and index finger millimeters apart, "to signing you up for online dating."

"Let's not go that far yet. After the holiday hoopla is over I'll focus on my love life."

After I move buildings and regain control of my life, then maybe I can invite someone in to it. Halle was happy for the holiday distraction Blake's offer brought … and for the relief of knowing she was getting the money she needed. She'd had the first decent sleep in awhile last night. Her life was starting to get back on track. Destiny awaited.

Chapter Two

Halle heard a knock on her door at precisely six thirty. *He's an on-time cowboy.* She took another look at herself in the mirror. *Hope I'm not over dressed—or under dressed. She touched the curls of her up-do. Maybe this was a mistake.* She sat on the corner of her bed while the second knock, a bit louder than the first, reverberated around the room. *What did I get myself into? I hate these things.* She was out of that life now and didn't want to go back.

She hadn't given much thought to her arrangement with Blake. There was no need—a few dates, play cordial, act normal, secure a business loan. Easy peasy. There was nothing fishy about it; it was a trade.

I'm out of my league. He's probably got a girlfriend. He's too good looking to be single. Maybe his family doesn't approve or, with the holidays, there's too much pressure for him with everyone expecting him to propose.

Halle stood, happy with her reasoning of Blake's motivation, and smoothed her hands down her red gown. She'd argued with Corrine about the strapless A-line chiffon, but in the end she'd lost. It did look good on her, and she had a necklace she'd made that matched it perfectly. She spritzed her favorite perfume, inhaled the vanilla and cinnamon scent, and headed toward the door.

. . .

Blake's jaw fell slightly when Halle swung open her townhouse door and he didn't know what to say. He'd expected to see the natural beauty he'd met at Just Dandy. Instead, he was face to face with a stunning woman in a red dress that hugged all the right curves. Her hair was pulled up but not like before. This time it had a purpose. He studied the smooth skin on her round face and worked his way down her sexy frame. *Wow.* Realizing his mouth was still open, he snapped it shut and cleared his throat.

"You look wonderful," he hurried the compliment so maybe she wouldn't notice his obvious gawking. *My family will certainly wonder about her.*

"Thanks, you too. I just need to grab my jacket."

He walked in as she turned and disappeared down the hallway. Blake had hoped to get through tonight, and the others, unnoticed. That was clearly not an option any more. *Damn, she's a looker.* He hadn't planned for her to clean up so well. His family was going to have more questions then he originally planned. All the better. Halle would keep them busy until well after New Year's.

He caught a glimpse of himself in a big mirror in her living room. He hadn't thought much about the tux he'd thrown on before coming over to Halle's—it was the one he always wore to these events. He lifted his hand to his cheek. *Good thing I shaved.* He'd almost decided against it. He was finding it hard to care lately. If his fate was already sealed at the bank, why should he try?

He glanced around Halle's place. She had a tan couch with white tables. The colors were light and airy—blues, browns, and some sage, rather like her store. It wasn't how most people in Wyoming decorated; no Western rustic charm to be found in the small living room. He liked it. Her place smelled of eucalyptus and citrus. He liked that, too.

"Ready?"

Her musical voice dragged him from thoughts of kicking up his feet on her couch and lying together while they watched television. *Except* Blake didn't watch a lot of television. He didn't have time. Nor did he ever think about *snuggling* with a girl on a couch or anywhere. He wasn't that kind of guy. Blake shook his head, as if that would get rid of his thoughts. *I need to get this night over with already.*

"Yep."

He stood behind her and helped her into an olive-colored trench coat as the scent of something spicy hit him. *Holy hell. She smells like a cinnamon roll.* He took a quiet, deep breath. Yep. Halle smelled delicious. This night couldn't get any worse.

Blake put his hand on the small of Halle's back and guided her to his black Ford F-350 King Ranch truck where he opened her door. She got into the high cab graciously and arranged herself before reaching for the seat belt. Blake noticed the gentle way she made sure her dress was tucked around her. It took him a moment to realize he was focusing on how her hands moved over the slippery fabric before he closed her door.

He slid into the driver's side and turned his key halfway; he had to wait a minute for the diesel engine to warm up every time he started it. Blake decided to capitalize on the forced pause.

"You're probably gonna get bombarded with questions." He shifted in his seat so he could face her. "If not tonight then the next."

"Bring it on." She turned toward him.

He suppressed the urge to squirm at the undivided attention. *Get over yourself Blake, this is a business deal. You do hundreds of these.* He couldn't, however, get over her eyes. They matched her trench coat and beckoned him closer. Blake wanted to lose himself in them. He resisted the temptation to reach out to her.

"So, what do I need to know?" she asked.

"For starters, if they ask if we're dating, say no." He'd been determined to stress this point, but now he wasn't sure that it was what he wanted her to say. He wasn't sure he ever wanted her to tell him no. "We're just long-time friends from high school." Blake forced the words. "That should keep them at bay."

"Which high school did we go to?"

"Casper High."

"Ah, so you're an Antelope, huh?" Halle chuckled then swayed her head back and forth. "I wish I would've known that from the start. I'm a Bronco. That's a deal breaker." She shrugged and turned, reaching for the door handle.

"Halle," he blurted out and reached for her arm.

"Just kidding … geez." A spark of amusement flashed in her green eyes when she twisted back around to meet his stare. "So we went to rival high schools. You, mister, need to lighten up." Her index finger shook a couple of times at him.

Blake released his grip when he realized he actually held her upper arm. He felt his cheeks warm, but refused to acknowledge an actual blush. He knew he was grumpy, he tended to get like that before these events. The obligation of it all pissed him off. He was fine once he got there; he liked most of the people.

"What happened to that guy who sat and drank with me in the shop in the middle of the day? He seemed fun." Her finger now pointed at him. "Frankly, you don't."

Blake blew out a loud sigh and turned the key all the way. He wanted to leave before she really did change her mind. He hadn't realized that option was even on the table.

"It's family. Lately, they've really been making me uptight." He glanced sideways at her. "That's why you're coming. It'll take the pressure off at these things, giving me a little more time to see straight to make a decision."

Halle's presence might initially bring questions, but in the long run would be worth it. December was a marathon of activities, not a sprint. No blind dates this season, no women unabashedly hitting on him, and he may even be able to deflect business decisions due to Halle. Blake felt a little bad using her, but she was getting something she apparently really wanted in return. They were even.

"Decision?"

"Yeah." He drove on so they wouldn't be late, side-stepping her question so he could return to his original point. "My mother will seem harmless—she's not. My dad will seem drunk—he is. My sister will seem nice." He paused. "She ... can be."

"Ah, big brother has a soft spot."

"How'd you know I'm older?" he asked as he braked for the red light.

"I can tell." She winked at him.

Tingles climbed his spine. Halle's sexiness level increased dramatically when she winked at him. *I might be in trouble.*

"Alright, well, keep your assumptions in check tonight."

"Please?" Halle's voice was soft.

"What?" he snapped.

"*Say please*. You can be nice. This is a favor, remember?"

"Yeah, favor." He sighed.

They were just two nice people helping each other out. *She's my fake date for the holidays. That's it.*

• • •

Halle was bored as the guests poured into the hotel conference room. She sat at the table designated for Blake's immediate family and drank her wine, watching all the well-dressed women saunter about. *Why is everyone in black?* Halle knew black was a classy color, but geez, have some imagination, people. She stood out in her red dress, and not just by her standards. *Good. I don't want to be one of these stuffy people anyway.*

She was used to talking with the people she hung out with, not politely nodding and saying inconsequential niceties like "I can't believe you manage all of that" or "I love your charity for the color orange, it truly is underrated." *How many of these events do I have left? Ugh.* Halle counted the days until Christmas Eve … twenty-four.

Good thing Corrine let me borrow dresses or this business deal would've cost *me money.* She drank more wine, enjoying its rich plum taste. It was an expensive treat she didn't get much lately and would be probably the only perk of these stuffy parties. *It's all for the loan. If this is what I have to do to get it, then so be it.* And, face it, Blake wasn't getting anything for free, either.

So, if she was going to get through this night and the others, she would have to try to have a conversation with someone. Maybe she should pick a group of women as her first target. Glass in hand, she prepared to unleash her sassy side. It was the only way she'd survive.

She stood, and straightened her red strapless gown and her necklace. She surveyed the room, moving from group to group. Lackluster. Too old. She finally settled on a group of women her age. If she was stuck here, she may as well try to get some business out of it.

Halle held her head high and plastered a pleasant grin on her face like the others—and like the others, she didn't mean it. She knew this type of crowd—the well dressed who usually judged on appearance alone. She'd had her fair share of run-ins over the years at these types of swanky events enough to know a group of stuck-up women when she saw one. As she drew closer to the group, acting as though she was going to walk past, one of them made eye contact with her.

"That is a beautiful dress," Halle complimented the stick-framed woman standing in front of her in—of course—black.

"Thank you." The woman acknowledged.

Halle feigned continuing to the bar when another woman spoke, welcoming her into the conversation.

"Didn't you come here with Blake?" the redhead asked too sweetly and then narrowed her eyes.

"I did." Halle maintained an even tone. *Hands off.* She had come here with Blake and that thought warmed her. Even if it was looking like this chick was a secret girlfriend. Halle took in a sharp breath. *What in the world am I doing? We aren't dating. He has a girlfriend.*

"How do you two know each other?" the woman persisted.

Halle studied the woman's inquisitive face. She was in her early thirties, maybe late twenties, and there was no ring on her finger. It appeared Halle wasn't exaggerating when she thought every single woman who knew Blake was after him.

Halle shrugged as if her answer was no big deal. "Old friends." She sipped her wine and tightened her lips. Did they not think she was good enough to be Blake's date? *Get a grip and just play their passive aggressive game.*

"Blake has a *lot* of old friends it would seem." She giggled primly.

"I'm sure he does," Halle spoke with her best innocent, agreeable voice, knowing the intended insult. "He's so nice and friendly, and a great listener, too."

Okay, so she was lying a little … well, a lot. But, it really seemed to irritate the woman and make the others in the group uncomfortable. So, she kept going. She'd probably regret it later, but right now, it was worth it.

"He gives the best advice, too." Halle sweetly articulated and then sipped from her glass again. She wanted to make them jealous but not get caught in a lie. It was a fine line. The less she said, the better chance she had to get away with it.

Another woman, who could be the twin to Ms. Asky Pants, piped up, "I heard he's been tapped to take his grandpa's place at the bank."

Work at the bank, huh? Halle pieced together the few conversations she'd had with Blake. *Oh, so he doesn't just have strings to pull. Maybe that's why he's so grumpy. He's a banker.*

Halle's gaze pursued the crowd, landing on Blake. From her vantage point it looked like all eyes were on him, which wasn't surprising. He was magnetic in a lone wolf kind of way. Halle tried not to stare, but it was hard not to. He looked dashing.

The women's laughter brought her back to the conversation she was attempting—poorly—to fit into.

"What do you think?" The pointy nosed woman with all the questions asked in true form.

"About?"

"Blake in a suit and tie for the rest of his life?" The woman laughed as if that were a joke. "Can you *even* imagine him running a bank?"

"Yes. I can." Halle felt her anger start at the tips of her fingers and move its way up to her cheeks. For some reason she didn't like these women laughing him.

She was getting ready to launch another round at the pesky woman when a beautiful woman in a gray dress joined the group. She was all dolled up with rich, curly black hair that fell to her shoulders. Halle greeted her and then narrowed in on the irritating, Blake-bashing woman.

"The bank would be lucky to have him. And whether he's in a suit or otherwise," she winked coyly, "he can wear *anything* ... trust me on that." She twirled on her bright purple open-toed pumps and headed toward the bar, leaving the women now sporting open mouths. *Suck on that.*

She got her drink, another red wine, and decided to grace Blake with her presence ... and another beer. She hadn't spent much time with him since they'd arrived, and part of their deal was that she accompany him around as he schmoozed. *Let's see what your world is all about, Blake.*

She sidled up to the group, her arm touching his sleeve. Without looking at him, she offered him the new beer. He turned and set down his finished one. In one fluid motion he brushed his finger tips over hers as he accepted the beer while his other hand smoothed on her lower back. All too quickly his finger tips and palm were gone, leaving only the flutters in his wake.

She scanned the group and recognized a face on the edge of the conversation. *Ramona?* Yes, that was Ramona Tillman. Society party throwing, volunteering to the max, charity chairing extraordinaire. *Crap. I should've figured I might know some of these people.*

Well, there was nothing to do except be proactive; it hadn't been that long since she'd seen Ramona. She waited for a break in the conversation and let Blake blanket her introduction to the group.

"Ramona, congratulations on the amount you raised for Military Moms. Amazing." Halle knew she could sing praises and Ramona would eat it up, forgetting to ask Halle things she didn't want to answer tonight or any night. She'd decided to give up the life of privilege because of the strings that came along with it. She was making a new way for herself now. There was no need to rehash her past … or for Blake to find out.

"Thank you, Halle. It was an event to remember. It's a shame you weren't there."

"Here's to next time." Halle raised her glass and then took a sip. She hoped Blake would view Ramona's statement as mere politeness. She'd been invited but had no interest in going—she understood Blake better than he knew. Halle just never had the foresight to strike up an agreement for a date to all the awful functions. *He's got better sense than I thought.*

Halle titled her head up to get a good look at Blake. His expression was a serene neutral until he turned to her. A smile played at his eyes and he fixed them on her. *How does he look so happy? I know he's not.* But she did know it was time to get out of this spot, even if she wasn't sure how to phrase their exit. They were supposed to be friends, so she had to keep her comments on the up and up to give off the correct vibe. *What's a friend-type thing to say?*

"I saw your sister over there." She nodded her head to the left. "I know you wanted to talk with her . . ."

Blake picked up quickly on the out she offered. He acknowledged the group and led Halle away by gliding his hand down her back, pressing the satin fabric onto her skin under his fingers, finally resting them dangerously low. Heat emanated from her lower back and she caught her breath. For a split second she thought his hand was going to keep going down ... not that she would've hated that.

• • •

"You aren't dating her?"

Blake furrowed his brows at his sister, Candace. "No. I'm not. Why do you keep asking?"

He pulled out her chair at the round table with dark green tablecloths, red ribbon, and a pine cone centerpiece with silver candles.

"She stood up for you to Angela. You should've seen it. Angela still has something for you, you know."

Blake squinted at his sister and sized up her black hair and thin frame wrapped in a shiny gray dress. He knew when something was off. "Spill, Candace."

"She also kinda made it seem like you two were more than friends."

"Did she now?" Blake smirked and drank his beer.

Candace's enticing news aroused urges he'd been suppressing all night. Halle looked extremely alluring in the red dress tonight;

very touchable. It took all he had to not sweep her up, kiss her, and spend the rest of the night ... not at a Christmas party. It was getting harder and harder not to think about her. He was a confirmed bachelor. He wanted to be left alone.

Blake had some serious choices to make about the bank presidency and where that left the ranch. He had no idea what he was going to do. And, really, it wasn't a choice. He needed to come to terms with his destiny. *Ah, hell.*

"I think you should date her. Mom already thinks you are."

His mother thought he was dating every woman he was ever seen with. "She hasn't even met her."

"Yet. She will before the night is out." Candace giggled and nudged him with her elbow. "Pretty ballsy, bro. You never bring anyone to these things and you expect everyone to think you are *just friends.*"

"I think you misunderstood what Halle was saying."

"Yeah, sure, okay." Candace rolled her eyes.

"Hi," Halle's voice came from his other side.

Blake swiveled his head to look up at her. "Hey."

She sat down before he could stand to greet her properly and laid her silver clutch in her lap.

"Candace. Sister." Candace nodded her head toward Blake but smiled wide at Halle.

"Oh." Halle's cheeks started to redden as she diverted her eyes for a moment.

Halle leaned forward, closer to him, and again he caught a whiff of cinnamon. *By everything holy in this world, why does she have to wear that perfume?* Blake was a man; he only had so much self-control. He clenched his jaw to squelch the heat rising in his body—he needed his blood to stay where it was.

Halle spoke softly to Candace, "I'm sorry about earlier. I didn't like what they were saying. And, it seemed to really get under their skin that I came with this one." She pointed her thumb to Blake. "So I saw an opportunity." Halle sat back in her chair.

Candace laughed. "Well done. They were pretty catty after you left."

Halle's a little spitfire. He couldn't help but like that about her.

Still, he made eye contact with her and gave her his best stern look. "I *thought* the plan was to lay low."

"You're *welcome.*" Halle glared back at him. "This is so unbelievably boring, Blake. It's not my fault they made me triple bitchy."

He couldn't help but smile at that convoluted reasoning. She was who she was.

"Blake, you should dance with this beautiful woman," Candace suggested.

Blake slowly turned his head toward his sister, eye brows raised. *What in the hell possessed her to say that?* Candace giggled. *Dancing.* He'd look like an ass if he didn't take Halle out on the dance floor. He was almost mad he hadn't thought of it himself. It was a sly way to hold her in his arms. And, if she'd already given the impression they were dating, this would just further that rumor. No need to squelch it now … it actually worked to his advantage. He started to rethink his original plan.

"You mean to tell me that *Blake Ellison* two steps?" Halle's question dripped with sarcasm.

"With that attitude you may never know." Blake matched her tone and even winked, using her own tricks against her. *Ha.*

"This night just got a whole lot more interesting." Halle stood. *Damn. She's taking me up on this.*

Blake took a healthy swig and set his beer down. Standing, he extended his hand to her. "Shall we?"

Halle's delight lit up her face as she took his hand. Her touch electrified every inch of him and tightened his chest. Blake wasn't expecting that. For a moment, he stopped breathing. A woman had never had this effect on him. *After the holidays I really need to quit drinking.*

They got to the dance floor just as Lynyrd Skynyrd's version of *Christmas Time Again* started. *Great. A slow song. Do we stand in one place? We could probably foxtrot to this.* As Blake weighed his options, his question was answered: other couples were swaying to the beat. *Dammit.*

Blake put his hand around her waist. Fleeting thoughts of pleasure danced to a different beat in his mind. *What am I doing?*

• • •

Halle relaxed into Blake's embrace. His hands were strong and he held her close. She loved this song and Christmas; the ultimate feeling of hope. The restlessness she first felt during the holidays gave way to the dream of what the new year would bring, and this year was going to be her best yet.

The glittered decorations in the room twinkled in the background as she focused on Blake's clean shaven face. She wasn't sure where else to look. His brown eyes watched her, his hands held her, and the sporadic contact of their bodies teased her.

Halle was surprised at the mixed emotions that heightened her senses. She kept expecting normalcy with him and kept receiving anything but. She wanted to know him. She wanted to talk to him. But, most of all, she wanted him to kiss her, to hold her closer.

She looked away from him, not willing to let him see her longing. *I'm in this for the money. No other reason. I don't like him and I don't need him.* Pretending was easy … not believing it was going to be the hard part.

Chapter Three

"Wow, the snow just keeps coming." Halle held tight to Blake's arm as they trampled through the snow that had fallen during the party toward his truck. She was trying to follow in the footsteps of a couple in front of them to save her shoes from excess moisture and her toes from freezing.

When they reached his black truck, Blake opened the door and helped her in. She expected him to close the door—a gentlemanly act she'd become accustomed to—but instead the door remained open and she heard, "You must be freezing. Are your feet okay?"

"Um ... yeah, they'll be fine. When I get home I'll dry them off and put some heavy socks on." *And sweatpants and snuggle with my heating blanket.*

She looked at Blake, but he was eyeing her feet. The sides of his jaw jumped slightly. Then, without saying anything, he opened the door behind her and started rummaging around.

"Whatcha doing? Can I shut this door? I'm freezing."

Halle had weighed her options of outerwear but had settled on what best matched her red dress, and that option wasn't insulated. The cold gave way to shivers and she started to rub her upper arms in a feeble attempt to warm herself. *I should've worn a heavier jacket. This is stupid.*

She rolled her eyes and, not looking, reached for the door handle—she could shut her own door, for crying out loud. Instead of making contact with the bar, however, her hand grazed Blake's cheek. Startled at the skin contact, Halle shot her head to the right just in time to see his brows furrow.

"Sorry. I'm cold. I was shutting the door."

"I have socks for you." Blake waved them in his hand. "Give me your feet," he commanded.

Halle didn't know what to say. She could put on her own socks, but Blake surely knew that. The sweetness of his actions hit her. A lump sat firmly in her throat. There was something about the tenderness in his eyes. Something about the way he knew she was cold and he was making the situation better for her without being prompted or asked outright. She didn't say a word; she couldn't. Instead, she shifted in the cold leather seat, moving her feet toward him.

Blake took off one shoe, and dried her foot with a rag she hadn't noticed in his hand. He slipped a big, thick wooly sock on her foot and pulled it up her leg as far as it would go. The sensation of his fingers deliberately sliding along her skin made her entire body scream. She wanted his fingers to keep going, past her knee to feel his hands on her bare thigh … and higher. Halle resisted the urge to squirm in her seat, a seat that was suddenly sizzling. His fingers retracted down her leg and it was all she could do to not yell "no" or reach out for him. He sandwiched her foot in his hands and rubbed them together like he was starting a fire with a stick. It was an unnecessary action; Halle was already burning up.

She was careful not to touch the wet floor mats with her newly dried foot as he moved on to the other foot. He repeated his steps and Halle's entire body responded with the same intensity. She watched his fingers move up her leg, holding onto the sock. For a moment, just a moment, she thought he might keep going. *Wishful thinking.* Halle breathed slowly as Blake moved his hands gently down.

Halle wasn't sure what just happened. Was that a plain act of kindness or was there more to it? She watched him use the rag to wipe the water off the floor mat the best he could, the expression on his face matter of fact. He hadn't looked at her once since she'd ran her hand into his cheek.

Blake touched a button on the edge of her seat and a soft orange light appeared. "The seat has warmers. That should help."

Blake shut her door and went around to his side, tossing the rag into his backseat. He turned his key, and Halle took the opportunity before the diesel engine fired up.

"Thanks," her voice was low and breathy. She still wasn't sure what happened. *Did that mean anything?*

Blake was an even keeled person, so it was hard to read him, but she was learning. On the dance floor tonight she'd thought she saw a spark in his eye and then this . . .

"Are you in a hurry to get home?"

"Um … no." All that was waiting for her at home was a pint of ice cream, her favorite holiday movie, and her sweatpants.

He turned his head and their eyes locked. "Want to get some hot chocolate and drive around looking at Christmas lights?"

The beauty of his brown eyes made her breath catch. "Yes," she answered excitely. She paused for a moment, her insides cart wheeling while she kept her face from reacting. *That was too eager. Be cool.* She didn't smile, blink, or move a muscle. If she didn't focus she may reach out and attack him with her lips and never let go. She cleared her throat. "Sounds like fun."

Blake nodded and focused on the road.

Halle loved hot chocolate, she loved Christmas lights, and she really wanted to spend more time with Blake; especially now. She was going to cozy up with her heated seat and hot chocolate and enjoy the decorations of the season. If she happened to find out more about her date and share a laugh with him; all the better.

• • •

Blake pulled up to the closest convenient store for hot chocolate—the hot chocolate he was committed to as well as driving around in the pursuit of Christmas lights. He wasn't sure what had come over him. One minute he was staring at Halle and her cold feet, the next he was drying them off and putting socks on them, and before he knew it he was asking her to basically stay with him a little while longer. Why did he crave this woman's company?

He wanted to have her on his arm at parties, nothing more. Their arrangement was gradually beginning to feel like a date. No. This was a business deal. *I'm helping her—or I will, and she's helping me.* Unfortunately, the line he'd drawn in the dirt was starting to blur.

He returned with the cups wrapped in their insulated sleeves. "It's not gourmet, but it's hot." He settled in his seat.

Halle shifted and drew his attention away from his outstretched hand holding the drink. She was sitting with her legs folded under the blanket he'd found in his back seat. Good thing he was always prepared … for winter and for warming up cold women. Well, for warming up Halle. He'd never done this sort of thing before. *I actually want to take care of her.* An unnerving chill swept his back. He wasn't in control of his feelings. *Damn that twinkle in her eyes.*

"Thanks." She took a tentative sip. "Ooh, you meant *actual* hot chocolate. No additives, huh?"

"That's it. I'm checking you into that recovery place over on Durbin tomorrow."

"Hmm." Halle giggled and took another sip, sighing as she snuggled more into the seat. "It's the simple things that make life great."

"I couldn't agree more."

He fired up his diesel and headed toward the east side of Casper. The lights in those neighborhoods were usually hung by hand and imaginative, showing the Christmas spirit instead of where Blake grew up, all put up by professionals and usually all white. If he and Halle were going to ooh and ah, they were going to do it right.

"Why did you start Just Dandy?" he crooked his head toward her.

She held the insulated cup of plain hot chocolate in both of her hands and for a moment he was jealous. Being firmly in Halle's grasp wouldn't be such a bad thing—he'd sure enjoyed it when they danced.

"Honestly?" She paused so long Blake was about to ask the question again. "I woke up one morning and thought *there's got to be more to life.* So I made a list of things I wanted to do someday and things I like to do. The end result became a store of assorted fun items; handmade, Western things that aren't found in a box store."

"You opted to be stuck inside on purpose?"

"Didn't you?"

"That's another story. Do you like it?"

"It's been an experience." She chuckled. "There's *a lot* more that goes into having a store than I originally thought." In a quick change of conversation she pointed out her window. "Check out at that one. Looks like they love green. A lot." Green bulbs outlined every line of a two-story home and two larger trees in the front yard. Deer and presents, lit in green, sat in between the two trees.

"Whoa. I don't think I've ever seen a blow up Santa wearing a green suit with a green sleigh. Ya think it's a statement on capitalism or their views on environmentalism?"

"That's a crap shoot." Halle rested her arm on the leather console between them.

Blake eyed her slender fingers, but squashed the itch to reach out and lock them into his. He pointed to a ranch style house on his side instead.

"And this neighbor thought he'd make up for it by using all red."

They both laughed. Blake caught himself. He hadn't felt this comfortable with someone in a long time—possibly ever. He wasn't trying to be the person he thought his family, employees, and investors wanted. He was himself, for better or worse. The women he usually dated thought of him as an Ellison, not a real person who might not care about the standing his family name brought. Halle didn't seem to care about any of that. He grunted a chuckled to himself. That wasn't the full truth. She did care … it was going to get her the loan she wanted. What surprised him was that *he* didn't care that's what she wanted from him. Women using him for what he could get them usually infuriated him. Knowing her cards were all on the table and she wasn't trying to play him put him at ease. He liked that about her. He could trust her.

He used his blinker and turned up a side road that looked promising. "Thanks for tonight by the way."

"I see why you wanted someone to accompany you to those things. They are brutal."

"Yeah. And you're not even trying to play the politics of it all. I wish some of them would wake up and realize there's more to life than their pettiness."

"You're singin' to the choir, baby."

Blake took in a quick breath and looked at Halle. She was sipping her drink looking out her window. *Baby. Was that a slip or the way she talks?*

"Choir, huh?" He chortled. He liked Halle calling him baby. "You have some strong feelings about the good ole boys in town?"

Halle shifted under her blanket. "Um … no. I was just commiserating."

"Well done. Thank you. I appreciate having someone on my side."

And she was definitely on his side. If Candace was right, Halle was already giving the stuck-up women at these things the what for on his behalf.

"That you will have for the next, what, four events?" She turned her head toward him and winked. "You may owe me more than a loan by the time we're done if they're all like this."

He blinked and grinned as he tried to concentrate on his driving. *Sonuvagun, she's pretty.* Blake reached discretely on his left side to make sure his heater seat was off—it was plenty hot enough in the cab. Halle made his heart flutter. Between that and the heat she stirred in him, he wasn't sure how to counteract it, or what to do about it.

"The next one will be laid back. It's at my family's ranch."

"Cool. I haven't been out to a ranch in years. Ya know, I've lived in Wyoming my whole life, except for college, and never ridden a horse."

"Really?"

"Yep."

"I have plenty out there. We'll have to go riding sometime."

After he said the words, they played back again and again in his head. His gut swirled. *Did I just ask her on a date or a friend thing?* He was getting way to comfortable with this woman.

"Yeah, that'd be fun. Maybe when the weather is a little nicer, though."

Thank goodness. Blake breathed a sigh of relief that Halle hadn't taken his off the cuff remark too seriously.

"No way! Stop!"

He pushed on the brakes. "What?" His eyes frantically scanned Halle.

"Look." She crunched forward and tapped her finger on the front windshield. "It's just like Christmas Vacation."

He pulled to the curb, his heart racing. The woman sure got excited about Christmas lights.

"Should we knock on the door to see if the Griswold's answer?" he joked as he leaned on the steering wheel to get a better look at the house lined head to toe with white lights, exactly like the holiday movie.

Blake delighted watching Halle's reaction to the different displays as they continued to mosey through the neighborhoods.

They created their own game, aptly titled Christmas Lights and the People Behind Them. Sometimes the decorating motif reasoning was a mystery to them, but it was always nice to laugh with someone and mean it. He got lost in her.

By the time Blake pulled up to Halle's townhouse, it was late enough that people were starting to turn off their lights. Sadness draped him, head to toe, as he put his truck in park. *I wish this night wasn't ending.* That thought struck up irritation. He had rarely ever wanted company to stay. *You'll see her again. She's a friend ... uh, business partner,* his newfound mantra replayed in his head. Blake cut the engine. The snow had piled up during their holiday light excursion, and Halle's walkway was nearly knee deep with snow. He walked around to Halle's door to help her down and opened it as she was folding the blanket.

"Come here." Blake outstretched his arms. Halle stared at him with her brows furrowed.

"Let me get you to your door without you losing a toe." He felt like a dork standing with his arms opened wide, offering to carry her inside. Maybe he should've thought this through a bit more. He'd made sure her feet were warm before and didn't want that effort to go to waste now. That was all. He was only being considerate. It was all business.

"I can walk." The words that came out didn't match the bright eyed look he was receiving. She wanted him to carry her, and he could tell she was enjoying his attention.

"No. Come here." He consciously rolled his eyes for effect. He didn't want to seem overly anxious to have Halle in his arms again. "Grab your stuff." He scooped her up before she could protest, barely giving her enough time to take hold of her purse.

Her perfume cut through the cold air and he gripped her tighter. *This is better than dancing with her.* Flares of intense need emanated from his arms, making him acutely aware of just how much he liked having Halle this close to him. Unlike the banquet, he let himself feel the emotions that were coming naturally. He twisted around, shutting the door with a soft back kick of his leg.

Blake peered down at Halle. She was staring at him, her eyes large with a peculiar look on her face. His gaze fell to her lips before he tore his eyes away to watch the path and make sure of his steps so he didn't slip.

Feeling her hands shuffle around his neck, he caught his breath. She was palm to skin on his nape and it burned … he wanted to feel her touch everywhere. *You don't need this right now.* Blake swallowed down the internal warfare conflicting his mind and body.

He stole another glance at Halle as he approached her front door. Intending it to be a cursory glance, he found himself lost in her deep, green eyes, unable to look away. Their faces were close … so close. *Keys … I need her keys.*

"Keys?" He put a gruff voice to his internal thought.

"Um, yeah . . ." Halle finagled her purse, fished around and presented a key ring with three keys on it. "The green one with dragonflies."

• • •

She watched as he located her house key and unlocked the door, all while keeping her safe in his arms. She closed her eyes for a moment, sure he wouldn't see her while he focused on the door. *Perfect ending to a perfect night.* Halle breathed in his evergreen scent that the snow seemed to make stronger. She could stay in his arms all night long. Maybe even forever.

But even without Blake in her bed tonight she'd sleep well with the memories of a fun-filled night, and a couple more yet to be had.

He pushed the door open and found the light, closing the door with his back. Disappointment dominated her emotions when he set her on her feet. That was quickly replaced with titters of excitement and expectation as it dawned on her that his hands were resting firmly on her hips.

Halle searched the barrage of emotion in his eyes. Her breath was more noticeable as her heart pounded and she couldn't focus. All she could think about were his lips . . .his lips that looked divine to kiss.

The moment spread out, neither one of them looking away. She felt his hands lift lightly and deciding that was her cue to back away, she turned toward her living room. *Holy crap, I was boxing him in. That's why he didn't move—he couldn't.* After she was sure there was a safe distance between them, she turned around to wish him a good night and thank him for the drive.

Blake was in the same spot; he hadn't moved at all when she found his eyes again. The same look was on his face and it was too ambiguous to read.

Halle didn't say a word. She didn't want to further embarrass herself. She was new to this situation, a guy just standing in her doorway, doing nothing. *Is he trying to figure out how to get out of here? He's right by the door.* The anticipation that was stirring in her turned to frustration. *Just turn around and use the door, Blake.* She smiled weakly at him.

As if reading her thoughts, he said a soft "good night" and was gone.

Chapter Four

Blake had to pick her up at Just Dandy, and there was no time for her to go home and change. This was the only event he seemed partial to when he'd listed them off the first day they met. Go figure it was at his family's ranch. Halle wasn't sure if it was a good old fashion hoedown or not, but he hadn't mentioned the need to dress fancy.

Winter was in full swing so Halle hedged her bets and grabbed a white, long-sleeved cowgirl shirt with gold paisley designs off her store rack and a comfy, navy blue sweater to go with it. She was already in dark jeans and her camel colored cowboy boots, so she slipped on the new shirt and wrestled her hair into a braid that wrapped around the back of her head and hung off her right shoulder.

Butterflies bounced around in Halle's belly. It'd been a long week without Blake. Which at first, hadn't been so bad until the feeling of his strong hands running up her leg was so intense she looked to make sure his fingers weren't actually there. She knew she had a problem when the way his eyes danced when he laughed his intoxicating deep sound started popping into her mind on a regular basis. She had to keep reminding herself—more often then she'd like to admit—that she could have fun, embrace the moment even, but she needed to keep a clear head about their business deal. And thinking about Blake's firm hands on her legs was not keepings her head clear.

The other holiday functions seemed like obligations, but this one appeared like fun. And Halle was happy about it because this was more her speed. Hopefully they would be real people who laughed when they found something funny and let you know when they were mad—not the fake types she'd met at the first party.

Blake was right on time, of course, and Halle closed up the store for the night. Once they were in the truck heading west, she asked, "How was your day?" She might as well—she had nothing else to say.

They were just friends, or merely business partners. Blake made that clear when he left the other night. It had bothered her, but by the time the morning light came, she was over it. He had a girlfriend anyway. This was never about dating—this was always about business. And that was alright by her. She needed the loan.

"My day was just dandy."

She turned her head toward him and chuckled. "Nice."

"I thought so." His grin was wide as he kept his eyes on the road. "It was fine. Full of meetings and whatnot. Same ole crap, just another day."

If he doesn't like his job or life why doesn't he just change it? She didn't understand people who felt trapped. Life was a series of choices, and if you didn't like the ones you're making, then change them. She had.

"How about your day?" he asked.

"Busy. The shopping season is in full swing."

More like booming—she'd looked over the numbers at lunch and she was ahead in her projections. Her family had many shortcomings … teaching her the ins and outs running a successful business had not been one of them. Thankfully.

"That's great. Still sure you want to move locations?"

"Yep. What do you need from me? Any other paperwork?"

"I shouldn't. I'll have your original application in hand soon and will approve it."

"*You* approve them?"

"A bank president has that authority, ya know."

"The *what*?" *He is the bank president?* This was a detail that had escaped her attention. She thought the women at the banquet were just gossiping. She hadn't paid attention to the position Blake was taking over at the bank.

"Is that so shocking?" He swiveled his head and looked at her with taunting wide eyes.

"No, but I didn't know you were that high up."

Blake was going to see her entire loan application. No collateral to offer and all. She resisted the urge to fidget in her heated seat. At least she hadn't put her dad's name on the application. *Will he put two and two together?* It didn't really matter. Blake probably wouldn't care who her dad was anyway. Halle had been slightly worried that something on his end of the deal would go south—now that she knew his position, it was as good as done.

"Believe it. It's my life." His eyes were back on the road and his face blank of emotion.

"If you're so unhappy then why don't you change it?" she snipped.

Blake didn't respond and Halle diverted her attention out of her window at the passing hills, trees, and patches of snow that hadn't yet melted. They rode in silence the rest of the way. That was just fine with her. She didn't want to talk about his fantastically bad life anyway. He didn't know problems. She had problems. She needed that loan to go through.

They finally arrived at the ranch, Blue Prairie, with its many buildings sprawled out for a couple miles.

"Holy smokes, Batman."

Halle leaned forward to take in the grand holiday scene in the country. White lights hung on the posts and two rail wood fences guided their path down the dirt road. Every other post held a simple green wreath with a red bow in the middle.

"It can really get ya in the mood."

Blake's matter of fact statement didn't begin to describe what she was feeling. This was Christmas. This felt like home.

"It's amazing," she whispered as she noticed the barns in the distance lit in different colors and penned areas holding a variety of animals.

At the end was a big cul-de-sac filled with ranching trucks like Blake's, some old and some new but all dusted with prairie. The main log house was two-story, rustic and grand, strung with multi-colored lights lining the ridges, windows, and wraparound porch. Halle wanted to run up and sit on the porch swing, snuggle in a blanket, and watch the stars for hours.

"The party's in here." He cut the engine.

Halle tore her eyes from the majestic main house to a red barn with white trim laced with red and white lights, and a gigantic version of the fence wreaths hung high on the hay door.

She accepted Blake's hand to get out of the truck. It was warm and big—her whole hand fit inside his. Bits and pieces of what she now called *the sock incident* floated through her mind. Her skin remembered his hands on her legs and she started to swoon. Instead of leaping into his arms, she planted her feet firmly on the dirt and crossed her arms to keep the cold out. She felt his familiar hand on her back leading the way as they headed toward the barn.

"Hey, Blake," a lean, older man called out from a finished wooden picnic table as Blake shut the barn door behind them. Halle noticed the difference in temperature instantly and uncrossed her arms.

"Frank." Blake tipped his head as he guided her to the picnic table to make introductions.

Halle shook the man's hand. "Nice to meet you."

"Now that's still up for debate, isn't it, darlin'?" Frank had a twinkle in his eye that she appreciated.

She laughed. "True. But, anyone who has Blake's respect has mine."

"Ah … and how do you know that?"

"A lady never tells." She demurely shook her head.

"Frank's been at the ranch since I can remember," Blake broke in.

They were sitting on one side of the table, Frank across from them. Halle couldn't help but notice that there was ample room on the bench, because they were the only ones on it, yet Blake was sitting darn near arm to arm with her. She bit into the side of her lower lip at the promise of what skin on skin contact with him did to her. She could smell Blake's deep forest aroma and she swallowed hard. *What would your girlfriend say about this?* Halle made a mental note to let Blake know she knew he had a girlfriend—he wasn't fooling her.

"Yet this is the first time I remember him bringing a lady out here." Frank's tanned face sized up Blake. "Tried to teach this boy a thing or two along the way. Don't think it ever sunk in though."

"Oh no, *no.*" A loud voice from behind Frank approached. "What are we talkin' about? Work? No. Not tonight. Tonight we talk about hunting and fishing and . . ." The jolly round man's gaze found Halle and proceeded to elongate his words, "Beautiful women. Why hello. I'm Roy." Roy bowed theatrically and came up smiling.

He's clearly been drinking. Halle liked the attention. These were harmless guys just having fun. She pushed the notion of the other stuffy events out of her mind. Tonight she was going to enjoy herself.

• • •

Blake took a deep breath. Roy was harmless—his wife was probably around here somewhere—but even so, Blake felt protective of Halle. He didn't bring her here to be ogled. He hadn't really needed a date to this function. This was just some ranch hands hanging out drinking beer. *So why did I bring her here?* He was scared of the answer.

"Grab us some beer, will ya?" Blake called after Roy.

"Us? Hmm." Blake heard a smooth male voice behind him. Great. Tony Watford, the lady's man who was a confirmed bachelor. "So I guess we know who you came with."

"I guess we do," Halle replied calmly to Tony.

Before Blake could say anything, Tony was sitting on the other side of Halle. A jealous pang seized his throat and he swallowed hard. *This bastard better not lay a hand on her.*

Tony was good looking. Blake was man enough to admit that. He'd seen the playboy in town at the bars, and women always responded to his looks and silver deviled tongue. But this wasn't the bar and this wasn't a random gal out for a good time. This was Halle. His date. *Dammit. Not date. I really shouldn't have brought her here.*

He drank the cold beer in his hands, wishing Halle's focus was on him and not Tony. He slid the other beer Roy had given him in front of Halle, touching the nape of her neck so she'd know it was there. He thought about keeping his hand there but removed it. He had no business keeping it there.

Music fired up from the other side of the barn and Blake turned to see Roy messing with equipment.

"May I have this dance?" Tony asked Halle.

Blake froze. *That sonuva . . .*

"Do you mind?"

Halle was looking at him, her head tilted slightly and her brows rose in question. *She's asking me for permission?* It took him a moment to realize he needed to answer. *Yes.*

"Nope." He shrugged and drank his beer. "Go ahead."

Halle and Tony sauntered to the dance floor that had been set up in the middle of the barn. They fox-trotted, two-stepped, and did every other silly country dance in the dirt. *Whatever.* Blake turned back to the table. He couldn't watch Halle laughing and smiling in that man's arms.

"She's a beaut." Frank watched Blake with knowing eyes.

"Eh." Blake took a long pull from his beer, glancing at Halle, trying to make it not obvious.

"Seems someone's a little jealous," Frank chortled.

"Who? Me? Nah."

"Son, I see the way you look at her ... and the way she looks at you."

"No. We're friends. Nothing more. We have a deal." Blake drank again, finishing his beer. He needed to do something to stop the rambling. At this rate he'd be drunk before the end of the song. "I just needed a date to holiday stuff. She agreed to tag along."

"Uh huh."

• • •

Halle had been smiling so much since they arrived that her cheeks were starting to hurt. Tony was light on his feet and the others were hilarious. The stories about ranching life kept her in high spirits most of the night. Even Blake seemed to loosen up. His easy smile was gorgeous ... his masculine face softened along with his mouth and Halle wanted to wrap her arms around him every time he laughed.

Everyone was gathered around the picnic table as Blake told a story about the first time he branded with Frank. Blake had been determined but still managed to get kicked and thrown around like a rag doll the entire week. Apparently the next year he wasn't much better. It wasn't until year four that he really figured it out, but the damage had been done and his reputation was sealed. His face was animated and his punch lines well timed—he even laughed with the others and casually drank his beer when Frank added his own not so flattering insights about Blake to the story. *Damn, I like this side of him.*

Tony had a nice face, too, she couldn't help but notice. *Nothing.* Her body didn't have the same reaction to Tony. She seemed to tingle only at the sight of Blake, his touch.

It was getting late and she yawned. From the three beers to the dancing and laughing, she was exhausted. She felt a hand on her lower back and melted into it. *Blake.* Halle let the tingles sweep through her and closed her eyes for a moment. His simple gesture made her want so much more.

Blake leaned in close to her, his lips almost touching her ear. "Tired? Ready to go?" he whispered.

Forget the simmering tingles. Energy bounced around every part of her and landed south. His low words, breath on her skin, and touch on her back sent her to a very awake cloud nine. She turned her head slightly toward his, causing their faces to nearly touch. He moved back a little before that happened. *Dangit.*

"Only if you are," she whispered back, looking into his brown eyes. They weren't just brown … they had flecks of gold in them that seemed to call her name. She wanted to lean into him, put her lips on his, and lose herself. Her gaze dropped to his mouth.

Blake pulled back, sat upright, and announced to the crowd, "Well, guys. We're calling it a night. Merry Christmas."

After exchanging well wishes for the holidays and the new year that was quickly approaching, they were on their way out the door, his hand never moving away from her back.

"Mistletoe," someone in the group shouted and laughter roared.

She looked up to see that right above the barn door hung a small cluster of mistletoe. A thrill shot straight up her spine to her throat. She brought her gaze back down and it landed square on Blake. *Is he going to kiss me?* He looked like he was contemplating life and was, once again, back to being unhappy about it. Halle wanted to crawl in a hole. Apparently, she wasn't mistletoe kissable.

"Afraid that's not gonna happen, boys. I'm not a PDA kinda gal," she tossed back. She'd saved face and now she couldn't reach the truck tucked away in the dark night fast enough. *This night ended on a low note. Thanks a lot, cowboy.*

Halle felt Blake's hand grab hers. She halted in midstride and pursed her lips together before whipping around. *I better get a lower interest rate.*

Blake was there, right there in front of her. She took in a quick breath. His rich evergreen smell enveloped her. *What's he doing?* Thrills swirled around in her midsection, extending outward until her entire being felt light. Before she knew what was happening or could voice words to ask, his hands were on her cheeks and his lips on hers. He was kissing her, deepening it with every moment. Halle relaxed into him, reaching out and finding his solid chest, then sliding her hands around to his back. Her excitement turned into fiery want … want she needed him to satisfy. Then, his lips were gone. She opened her eyes, staring back into ones that were full of desire.

Blake turned and faced the barn door. Putting his hand on the small of her back, he prodded her forward. She may not have moved otherwise. *Blake just kissed me and in front of people.* The words sounded off in her head then repeated themselves freely the rest of the night.

He raised one arm as they left and waved to the group that had been—surprisingly enough—stunned into silence. They weren't the only ones.

"Good night, ya'll."

Chapter Five

Blake pulled up to the North Platte River Bank, sat in his truck and stared at the front door. People strolled in and out on an uncharacteristically sunny and warm morning for December. *This is my future.* He put his hand up to his chin and rubbed it while he leaned back in the leather seat of his truck. *Maybe it won't be so bad.* He watched a women with three kids in tow fight them into the bank. *Ah hell, who am I kidding? For the rest of my life I'm going to be tied to an office.*

Blake had been the interim bank president for five weeks. Five. Weeks. He couldn't remember one day that he went home thinking *yep, this is what I want to do forever.*

He grumbled as he ambled out of his truck and to the top floor of the bank. He'd much rather be baling hay, hauling hay, or feeding hay to his horses. He belonged outside. *You'd think in my family I'd get to do what I wanted.* He stewed on that as he said his morning pleasantries. It wasn't the people he didn't like. They were fine. Some of them were even great. No, it was the job. He didn't like being in a stuffy office all day talking about numbers. At one point, the life of an accountant sounded ideal. His finance degree and MBA even made it seem lucrative, in theory. But the practice sucked. The life of a banker, accountant, or even president of a bank was nothing more than a glorified bean counter. Hell no. Now, he couldn't seem to muster the ambition for four walls.

His grandpa had entrusted the bank to him, and Blake knew why. They'd always shared a passion for finance and helping people with loans. Blake had grown up with his grandpa by his side both on the prairie and in the office, two passions they'd equally shared. It had been a great mix: during the week they worked hard inside and the nights and weekends were spent sweating outside. He loved his life. Since his grandpa's death eight weeks ago, Blake couldn't seem to find that light anymore. It all seemed pointless. He wanted to be on the open range. He wanted the blue sky above him, not fluorescent lights.

Worse yet was now his father controlled most of the Ellison assets. He'd never hit it off quite right with his father. His grandpa had been more like a dad to him—they'd shared the same interests, had the same way of thinking, and had always respected the other's opinion. His father on the other hand? All he respected was the bottom line. *There's more to life than money.* Blake had long since given up hope on having what others had with their dads. He took solace in the fact he had that with his grandpa. Well, he'd *had* that.

"Mr. Ellison, here are your morning reports." Nina, his assistant, placed a stack of papers and his morning coffee on his desk.

"Thank you," he said to her back as she scurried out of his office.

Some parts of the job weren't so bad. The morning dark roast filled his nose and his eyes seemed to open a little wider. His first order of business: find out why in the heck Halle's application had been denied. Surely there'd been a mistake.

He picked up the phone and dialed the loan department extension.

"North Platte River Bank, loan department, this is Agnes, how can I assist you today?"

"Agnes, it's Blake. How's your morning going?" He grinned because he'd always been partial to Agnes. He remembered when she started; she'd been the first hire his grandpa had let him help with.

"The sun rose and so did I. It's a great day."

He laughed. She always had something catchy to say.

"I was calling to get Halle Adams' loan application. Apparently it has already been denied and I wanted to take a closer look."

"Sure thing, just give me a second . . ." He could hear fingers tapping on the other end. "Well, there's a note here . . ." her voice was hesitant. "I can't access the file."

Why would her file be flagged? He realized he still didn't know much about Halle, and this mystery was just more proof.

"What does the note say?" he asked.

"It says you need to speak with Mr. Bowman."

"That's all it says?"

"Yes, sir."

"Alright, Agnes. Thanks for checking." He paused. "May the moon come out to kiss you good night and hold you safely in its heart and sight." Blake heard giggling and "ah, Mr. Ellison" on the other end as he hung up the phone.

Why did Jerry limit access? He couldn't remember when he'd ever been denied anything at the bank. Was there a legal issue with Halle's application? Personal information that needed to be locked up for some weird reason? He grumbled.

Blake tried not to let frustration get the better of him. Was nothing simple anymore? Why couldn't people who needed a loan get a loan? Why couldn't people change their dreams? Why had he kissed Halle?

Boom. That was his real problem. That was the question that had been haunting his every waking moment, and most of his dreams, for the last two days. Kissing Halle was the closest he'd ever come to an out-of-body experience, or what he figured one felt like. His arm was grabbing after her and his hands found her face and his lips set on hers. His anatomy had decided to kiss her, not his mind. Now, his mind wouldn't let go. Halle had felt so soft under his lips, so inviting. She'd kissed back; there was no denying that. Halle had caressed her lips over his and reached out for him, pulling him closer. The memory fired up Blake's skin starting at his lips and working downward. He wished Halle was with him now. If she were, he didn't think he'd be able to stop at one kiss.

She hadn't said much on the ride home. She'd sat silently and looked out her window. At what, Blake wasn't sure. It'd been pitch black outside.

Blake had clearly overstepped his bounds. He blamed it on the moment and the dumb mistletoe for lending him an excuse. He blamed it on his stupid jealousy and seeing Halle thrive in the environment he coveted the most. She'd kept her own with the guys and they'd taken to her. The whole night had led to one big mistake that had screwed him over. And he wasn't quite certain how far his misstep reached.

Blake got back on the phone and dialed Jerry. Instead of a real Jerry, he got a recorded Jerry and left a message at the beep.

• • •

Corrine stopped fussing with her sewing project and lifted an eyebrow. "Say that again."

"He kissed me." Every time Halle said it she bit the side of her bottom lip to keep from gushing like a schoolgirl.

She wasn't sure what had happened. They were in the clear with the guys, they could've walked away. But Blake had still laid one on her.

Neither one spoke much on the way home. Halle wouldn't have minded conversation, but she couldn't come up with much to say that didn't involve some version of *hey, you just kissed me— why? Do ya wanna go steady or somethin'?*

"He kissed you in front of everyone?" Corrine asked.

"Uh huh. But it wasn't one of those fancy parties. We were out at a ranch his family owns."

"Still."

Halle had broken down and told Corrine who she'd been going to parties with. She still played it off as if they were old friends—a friend she'd never mentioned to Corrine in five years. Halle just had to tell someone. She had to give the account of the night out loud so that it was real ... because it was.

"Maybe you're not in the friend zone anymore." Corrine got back to sewing.

"Nah." Halle shook her head. "I think we are."

Does that kiss bring this whole thing to the next level? Like, friends? She took a deep breath. She didn't know what the kiss made them. But she did know they avoided talking about it after, and that didn't feel like a good sign.

"The kiss was fantastic though." She returned to browsing through the racks of clothes at Dress to Impress. "I think the next thing is political. I should probably be ultra conservative." Halle glared at Corrine. "Nothing strapless."

"I've got just the thing." Corrine cleared her lap of fabric, stood, and headed toward the back where she kept extra inventory. "Be careful, Halle. It sounds like you like him," she called out.

Yeah, I should be careful. This business arrangement was getting complicated, Halle reminded herself for the umpteenth time. Maybe this could turn into a friendship. Not dating. Surely he had a girlfriend. *And, if that's how he acts when he has a girlfriend then ... geez, no thank you. I don't need that mess.* She needed her loan to get approved so she could move out from under her father's thumb once and for all. Halle straightened herself and held her head high as she followed in Corrine's footsteps to see what she had in mind. *It better be classy.*

Chapter Six

Where's Halle? Blake nodded to the bartender for a beer, shoved his hands in his black jean pockets and spotted Halle twenty feet away. Halle and Candace laughed like old friends on the other end of the open bar at the Christmas party for all of the bank branch employees. Halle's curly hair bounced on her shoulders as she used her hands to emphasize her words. She looked so touchable. And kissable.

They'd been separated when he'd commanded the floor to welcome the bank employees and their families and thank them for a wonderful year. He'd damn near choked up when he started to talk about his grandpa. Then, he'd searched the crowd and locked onto Halle's watery green eyes. Somehow, down deep, her face—that single moment—had given him strength to finish his story without blubbering like a fool in front of hundreds. Now, all he wanted was a replay of the mistletoe scene. His gaze flitted across the room. *Damn. Every party should have mistletoe.* He picked up his beer and started to walk toward the only person he wanted to talk with.

"Nice speech." Gordon Ellison stepped in his path.

"Thanks." Blake let the cold beer splash down his throat to give him a couple seconds to figure out why his father had seemingly sought him out.

His father looked over his shoulder then back to him with a knowing smile. "That the girl?"

"Yep." Blake didn't like where this conversation could go. *Now I remember why I don't bring dates to these things.* He put his free hand back in his pocket. His father reeked of whiskey.

"Pretty."

Blake didn't say anything. He only stared. They didn't talk about women. His father had never showed much interest in his life in general; only business. Irritation flooded Blake's head. *Is he seriously trying to show interest in my life right now?* His father couldn't replace his grandpa if that's what he was trying—poorly—to do.

"How's the portfolio?" His father's position as the executive director of the Ellison assets put his hands in everything—everything but the bank. His grandpa had always kept that separate. He'd always ear marked the bank for Blake it seemed. *Thank you, Grandpa.*

"I've contacted a few buyers who have shown interest over the years in the ranch." He jingled the ice in his stubby glass. "I should have it sold by January."

"You can't just sell it." Blake smelled the familiar cinnamon that accompanied Halle as she joined them and instinctively put his hand on her back, but instead of merely resting it he slid it around to hold her waist close to him. Under different circumstances he would've let the sensation of her curves rubbed against his body sink in.

"Yes. I can."

Blake turned to Halle, working to keep his expression neutral. She didn't deserve the full brunt of his anger. "We're leaving."

He was not having this conversation with his liquored-up father tonight. He was having a good time and just wanted to enjoy seeing Halle again. It had been an exceedingly long week since he'd seen her last. Of course his father would turn a perfectly good night sour in a hurry.

Halle searched his eyes and, without saying another word, ambled with him through the crowds of people, deftly avoiding any conversations.

The sad thing was this time Blake had actually raised his expectations. His holiday obligations weren't so annoying with Halle by his side. Halle. The woman who still didn't acknowledge the kiss between them, which forced Blake to pretend it didn't happen either.

The fact that he brought a date to the functions seemed to be keeping his family in check—or rather *was* keeping his family in check.

"What was that about?" Halle questioned after he pulled out of the parking lot.

"Nothing." Blake growled.

The last thing he wanted to do right now was explain. He sped up to get Halle home quicker. *I want to be alone.*

"Come on," she prodded. "The thing with your dad."

"It was *nothing.*" He hoped the edge in his voice was clear. *Another one down. I can't wait for this month to be over.*

"It didn't *look* like nothing," she said, her concern obvious. "It definitely looked like *something.*"

"Frankly," he looked at Halle and then back to the road, "It's not *your* business. It doesn't concern you. If it did, then I'd tell you."

There was silence. *Just perfect. Now I'm the ass.* Blake huffed. He stuck his chin out slightly. *I'm right though. She's still practically a stranger.* A stranger he wanted to kiss and tell his innermost thoughts to, but only an outpouring of jumbled words would come out right now if he tried to explain himself. It wasn't going to happen tonight.

The stillness stretched for blocks. He rubbed the back of his neck and pressed his lips together. *She doesn't deserve my attitude.* He glanced at her again. The street lights rolled over her face in the darkness. She was looking straight ahead. His side view of her beautiful face gave no indication she was happy. *At least she cared enough to ask.*

"You don't need to worry about it is all I meant," his soft words elicited no response from her. "It's something I have to deal with," he tried again. Apparently it was still a no-go, based on the oppressive silence in his cab.

He pulled up to her townhouse, cutting the engine. He didn't want to look at her. She was upset, and he detested dealing with crying women. Ever since he had met this woman, his life was one big rollercoaster.

"Halle." He shifted now, deciding he had no choice. He sighed—he hated it when he didn't have a choice.

She looked at him, her eyes and face cool, devoid of emotion. Her lips were pursed together and she squinted at him. She still didn't say a word. Instead she gathered her clutch and opened her door.

What in the hell? This scenario was new to him. Usually when he was a prick, there was fighting, crying, or screaming— some emotion that usually made him want to throw himself into oncoming traffic. But apparently Halle was proving not all women were highly emotional. He didn't know that type of woman existed. But was that a good thing? At least with the others he knew where he stood.

Loss filled Blake's throat. He couldn't squelch his urge to know his status with her. It bubbled up inside him to the brink. He swallowed hard as he watched Halle's determined steps make their way to her front door.

Dammit. He rushed out of his truck, his heart pounding rapidly. He had to reach her before she disappeared behind her front door.

"Halle," he called out.

She finished unlocking her front door and whirled around. "Yes?"

Her green eyes were firm and unwavering. Blake took in a deep breath of crisp air. Should he kiss her? Could he get away with that? Would it be like the movies and they'd live happily ever after?

"I'm sorry."

"For?" Her eyebrows rose.

"Um…" *Does she seriously not know?* "Earlier." He pointed behind to his truck with his thumb. "I shouldn't have said that."

"Was it not true?"

What is your game, woman? Blake scratched the back of his head. He was in some kind of twilight zone.

He chortled; he didn't know what to do. "It *was* true. You just didn't deserve it put like that. I'm sorry. I don't usually talk about those things."

"Maybe you should." Halle walked into her place.

"Are we still on for next week?"

She narrowed her eyes at him and closed the door.

Was that a yes?

• • •

"You should've seen his face when I shut the door." Halle shook her head retelling last night's events to Corrine in Just Dandy.

"I can't believe you didn't say anything to him." Her quirky friend leaned on the glass counter.

"He was kinda right," she continued, adding her newly made necklaces to the glass case. She'd made a lot of the pieces last night to deal with her frustration. "I mean, it's really *not* my business."

"Still."

"Yeah, I wanted to rip his head off, but where would that have gotten me? Nowhere. And I need to go somewhere. Across town to be exact . . ." Halle's voice trailed off.

Corrine cocked her head and furrowed her brows. "What are you talking about?"

In all the girl talk, she kept forgetting she hadn't told Corrine the entire story. She didn't even know Halle had applied for a loan the first time. She didn't want to say anything until she knew for sure, which turned out to be wise since the loan didn't go through. Now that the loan was going to happen, she had to tell her friend they'd no longer be store-mates. That moment didn't feel like now.

Halle shrugged, trying to play off her misstep. "Across town. The next thing is across town. I can't believe we are almost halfway through December."

"You still gonna go to these things?" Corrine straightened, held a pair of pink chandelier earring up to the sides of her face and looked into the mirror on the counter. "I don't care how long you've known him, he sounds like an ass."

"No, he's not; not really. I think I hit a nerve."

Halle knew about Blake's type of family life and how stressful it could be. There were standards to be met and someone always telling you what to do. She didn't blame Blake for being irritated, although she didn't think taking it out on her was necessary. She pursed her lips to one side. She'd been naïve to think they were in the friend zone and he'd talk to her, as if she were someone special to him. She sighed and returned to displaying her necklaces.

Things with Blake may be stationary, at best, but her relationship with her dad wasn't. She was dreading the call to tell him that she was moving her store to a new location. It would be satisfying to say the words—that was a fact—but he'd try to talk her out of it, then get mad and they'd fight. That was their cycle.

"Hey, what did you say he looked like again?" Corrine reached for a candy cane from one of Halle's display Christmas trees in the front window.

"Tall, dark, and handsome." *So handsome.* She slid the last necklace into the case and remembered the feeling of Blake's hand on her back, tender yet commanding. *Mmm.* She melted at that simple act every time and didn't think she'd ever view something so effortless the same again.

"'Cause I think he's here."

Halle's head shot up. "What?"

"He's coming in!" Corrine rushed to the counter and tried to look nonchalant in her yellow track suit just as the front door jingled.

Within seconds, Halle found herself face to face with her date—no, business partner—from last night. His brown eyes were fixed on her, intense and demanding. Her stomach fluttered and a streak of adrenaline prickled the tips of her fingers.

"I thought I'd find you here," Blake's voice was calm and collected.

"Savvy." Halle kept her tone light; she felt anything but. Her heartbeat quickened as Blake's familiar scent soaked into her senses.

"Listen, about last night." He tousled his ball cap, scratching his head. "I wanted to make sure you and I are still on for our deal."

Their eyes locked and she searched his. She wasn't completely sure what she was looking for, but as she explored, his face relaxed, he was no longer grinding his teeth, and his eyes looked at her differently … almost with desire. No, that couldn't be. Surely she was projecting. He was the same jerk from last night.

This is for the business loan. Halle suppressed her urge to say no, their deal was off. Okay, so she wasn't a part of his world—he was the one who had invited her. And no, they weren't friends. But, just because they weren't didn't mean they couldn't be. She wasn't going to blab his business around town; the same as she expected from him.

Halle hadn't told anyone about her need for a business loan. *Including Blake.* She'd gotten so caught up in the not-dating situation; she hadn't realized her own reticence. *I guess we're more similar than I thought.* A smile tugged at her lips. *I just hide it better.*

She reigned her amusement into a small grin and held his gaze. "Yes. We're still on."

...

Blake let out the breath he didn't realize he'd been holding. That was good news for more reasons than just the obvious. The thought of having to attend these functions alone made him want to vomit.

"Thank you," he said in his sincerest voice, and meant it.

He liked being around Halle. She heightened his senses and made everything better, even lame holiday events. Blake liked that he felt envied with her on his arm. Having already experienced an elevated social stature his whole life, he wasn't sure what this new pride was about. But, now ... now he felt like they were finally right. Except it was all a lie. They weren't together. Blake breathed in and Halle's cinnamon scent soothed him. He was looking forward to the next event. That, he realized, hadn't been the case in many years.

"You must be Blake." A soprano voice came from his right.

"Yep." He pulled his gaze away from Halle. "And you are ... ?"

"Corrine."

The woman, who looked to be in her fifties, extended a dainty hand for him. He shook her limp grip, stopped himself from outwardly cringing, and braced himself on the counter with his left hand.

"Corrine owns the dress shop next door," Halle spoke up. "She supplies me with all my wardrobe choices."

"Very well done then, Corrine. Halle always looks . . ." He let his passionate gaze drift over every inch of Halle. "Great."

"Since she's decided to still go to these things with you—why I'm not quite sure," Corrine pursed her entire face, "maybe you two should match for the next event. What is it again?"

"A political thing at the theatre," he answered before the words registered. *Match?*

"Oooh, artsy. Hmm," Corrine tapped her finger on her chin.

"I was thinking this event might suit the lacey dress we picked out the other day," Halle suggested.

Lace? Um, yes, please! He braced himself at the thought of her bare skin under lace. He appreciated how the dresses showed off her figure ... her beautiful, round curves that he had to focus on not focusing on every time he was around her. Standing in her shop now, she looked just as pretty in jeans and a black turtle neck. He still wanted to reach out for her and ... his gaze dropped to Halle's full lips.

"That is perfect for the theatre. I think I have something Blake here can wear . . ."

"Hold the phone. Matching?" He quizzed Halle because she was clearly the sane one of the two.

"Corrine, Blake is a big boy. He can wear whatever he wants," she told her friend, who didn't look happy at that news.

"When couples . . ."

Halle spoke loudly to Blake, cutting Corrine off, "You don't have to wear anything to match my dress."

Corrine glared at Halle but looked sweetly at Blake. "How about I go get it and then you can decide?"

"Sure," he replied.

What's the harm? He had other pressing matters to ponder. If he hadn't showed up today would she have cancelled their deal? Okay, so Halle had been mad at him. That's justifiable. He understood that she didn't jump for joy at the thought of these ball-busting events. Hell, he didn't even want to go—which is why he'd stuck up the deal with her in the first place.

He stood across from Halle now and wasn't sure what to do. He pretended to be fascinated by the shelves of plaques with quotes on them. They were still on for the Christmas parties, so that was a good thing. She was going to keep dressing up, which excited him. What else should he say to her?

He was about to open his mouth about the weather when the back door flew open and Corrine appeared with a Christmas boutonniere to match Halle's dress. He took the box and counted his blessings he wasn't in the middle of any pathetic spiel asking Halle out for real. Still, knowing he wouldn't see Halle for six more days didn't put a smile on his face as he thanked Corrine and left.

Chapter Seven

Halle walked into the Blair Sonora Theater with Blake by her side, guiding her with his palm. The magnificent foyer of the old theater was decorated in grand reds, silver, and gold. There were Christmas trees tastefully placed with giant nutcrackers and other garland accents. The room was filled with people in black tuxedos and dresses. *Of course, they're all in black.*

Halle was suddenly very glad she'd picked out a conservative bronze colored dress, with a little flare. She couldn't completely give in and lose herself. Her dress had lace sleeves and lace that covered shiny fabric in that same color to her knees, leaving her orange strappy heels to be beautiful all on their own. She completed her look with dangling earrings that matched her shoes, her blonde hair in ringlets that swayed above her shoulders.

She knew it was silly, but she sensed all eyes on her. She was Cinderella and Blake was her prince. *A prince who wore the matching boutonniere.* She grinned politely at the crowd, not focusing on anyone in particular.

Blake nudged her to the right toward the bar directly in their path. *At least we're both on the same page.*

Of what book, she wasn't so sure. Feelings and facts starting to get muddled in her mind. One minute she was focused only on owning a building and the next she was day dreaming about vacationing with Blake in the tropics. His tall figure sun-kissed and half naked…

She tried not to picture their beach romping as they approached the counter. Her life was a hot mess. How she got herself into these situations she had no idea ... they just seemed to happen and before she knew it she was traveling full speed ahead to an epic fail. Well, not this time. She knew what *she* was doing and why. What Blake was doing was of no concern to her.

"Wine?" he asked.

"Yes, *please*."

Blake eyed her.

"Blake, baby, I didn't see you arrive."

They both turned around and were met by Blake's mom.

"Just got here."

Halle watched Blake's demeanor shift from cranky to almost cheery. He flashed his perfect smile and the transformation was complete, even to his eyes. *This man knows how to turn the charm on and off instantly.* Halle made a mental note of this known, but newly witnessed, skill.

"Halle. Nice to see you again." The older woman with perfectly set white hair focused her attention on her. She resisted the urge to fidget under the inspection.

"You, too, Mrs. Ellison." Halle had been able to avoid anything more than pleasantries with Carol Ellison so far, with a little over a week left in December, it seemed her luck had run out.

Carol spoke to Halle but stared disapprovingly at Blake. "I'd like to say I've heard a lot about you but, as I'm sure you know, my son doesn't divulge much." Carol's face was stern and her eyes squinted at him.

"Well, he's told me a lot about you." Halle demurely lied. "Your foundation to help foster kids is inspiring. I don't know how you are able to juggle everything."

Halle took her drink from Blake and clenched it. *Keep being overly sweet.*

"Thank you, my dear. It seems, Blake, you have found yourself a sweet one." She sized up her son and seemed pleased with his appearance. "Make sure you speak with Senator Davis tonight, will you." Her question was posed as a directive.

Someone called for Carol's attention and just as surprisingly as she arrived, she left.

Meanwhile, Blake was surveying the room coolly with one hand in his pocket and the other on his beer. The tux was identical to the one he wore at the first banquet and he looked good. Every single damn day the man looked effortlessly good. *What's so bad about this life for him? He fits right in.*

At least he has an ally in his sister. Halle was an only child. She never had the luxury of calling a sibling to complain or have them back her up when things got rough. She didn't envy Blake's life, she knew it all too well, but she did envy that he had a sister. Candace seemed pretty great. Blake had told her that they had always been close—standing up for each other when sometimes it was them against the entire family.

"Did I handle your mother acceptably?"

Blake's eyes were brilliant when he turned them on her. "Perfect."

Halle was now the recipient of his grand smile, and it unnerved her. *He is impossibly handsome.*

"Mom is so mad right now." He chuckled and drank his beer. "She's very passive aggressive. That was her way of chastising me for not keeping her in the loop about you."

"What kind of game are you playing with your family?" Halle couldn't stop herself from asking. *What did I get myself into?*

"Their game." The smile was still on his face. "I'm just playing their game."

That's it. She couldn't take it anymore. *I'm not the one who should be navigating this world.* "You really should've just brought your girlfriend."

Blake looked puzzled and opened his mouth to speak when the lights of the foyer started to dim, signaling the crowd into the theater and ending their conversation. Blake placed his hand on her back, a motion she was coming to expect ... and crave.

• • •

The play about love, Christmas, and magic was long and tedious. And when it ended, they shuffled out with the masses. So far he'd managed to have spoken only to his mother, and the look on her face was priceless. She obviously thought he was dating someone and she was the last to find out. *Ha, I couldn't have planned that any better if I'd tried. Joke's on you, Mom.* He shouldn't act like this, especially to his mom, but he was mad about his family trying to control his life and the fact that they didn't know much about Halle was probably his twisted way to get back at them.

Blake's goal was to have a quick word with the senator, the only reason he was here in the first place, and then make a beeline for the door. He surveyed the crowd. The senator was an equally tall man and finding him in a crowd was usually not a problem. Blake felt his sleeve rustle. His heart rate quickened before his mind realized who it was. *Halle.* He took a deep breath. Why had she surprised him? Of course she was right next to him. He could smell her intoxicating scent; she'd changed it tonight, but something was still the same.

There he was. His eyes settled on Paul Davis, the man of the hour.

"Let's go say hi to Senator Davis," Blake spoke low as he ushered Halle toward the man. "His wife is Veronica. She is big into animal foundations. My family has been close with them for as long as I can remember. I just need to chat a moment, then we can go."

At that moment, someone moving past them bumped his hand lower on Halle's back, down to the fullness of her butt. Blake's heart rate kicked up a notch as he returned his hand to its former position. His gaze dropped to where his hand just caressed. He couldn't help it. Halle looked amazing in her bronze dress. She always looked good—jeans, dresses, it didn't matter. He steadied his breathing to control his physical reaction to her and her curves. *Get a hold of yourself man.* He still had business to conduct. And Halle clearly wasn't interested in him. She barely made eye contact with him all night and still seemed less than thrilled to be there. Not that he could blame her on the latter.

He cleared his throat and reached out to shake Paul's hand. "Good to see you."

"Blake. It's been a while."

"How'd ya like the play?" Senator Davis asked after the round of obligatory introductions.

"Well, Senator, I thought it was as good as your duck hunting skills," Blake razzed the man he'd known since grade school.

"Yes, I thought it was magnificent as well."

The men chuckled and the women rolled their eyes.

"I swear, the more I work to save animals, the more he kills." Veronica directed her retort to the group but snickered with Halle.

"It's called relating to the constituents, dear."

"I've heard of your work with animals," Halle admitted to Veronica. "Don't sell yourself short, you do *a lot* of good. I envied the anti-animal testing laws you helped pass."

"Hey, I had a little something to do with that," Paul weighed in.

"Yah, writing that signature is heavy lifting," she shot back good naturedly.

Blake marveled at how Halle always seemed to know what to say. He'd witnessed her holding her own in all types of situations over the past couple of weeks. She never faltered, even when Blake suspected she had no idea what she was talking about. *She's crafty. I'll give her that.* He could use a woman like that on his arm all the time. Halle could be the sociable one and he wouldn't have to worry about coming to these things anymore. *What am I thinking? This is ridiculous.*

"You'll have to come down to the center, we'd love to have you," Veronica capitalized on Halle's feigned interest. "We need volunteers for all sorts of things."

"I'd love that." Halle's eyes lit up. "I have a weak spot for all creatures."

Huh, I didn't know that. How is it she knows more about me than I know about her? That thought disturbed him. He prided himself on keeping his life to himself. How had he told her as much as he already did?

"Oh, dear, that is Mr. Dempsy." Paul's gaze adverted as he reached for his wife. "Didn't you want to catch him?" She nodded, clearly having moved on mentally to the next conversation for the evening. "Blake, great to see you. I'm in town after the holidays. I'll call you."

"Sounds good. Merry Christmas."

He turned to face Halle as the couple sought out Mr. Dempsy.

"That was it?" she said.

"Yep."

"Aren't you offended?" Halle's brow furrowed.

"No. I've known Paul for years. That's what he has to do. When he comes back to town we'll get together and have some beers, kick back. I just had to formally say 'hi' here more or less to make my mom happy."

She seemed confused and that caused Blake to grin. She was so naïve to the world that was second nature to him. All of these events were really about glad-handing and appearances for the most part.

"I'm not seeing anyone, you know," he blurted out the words. "No girlfriend. I'm not sure where you got that from." He had no plan for what to say from there, and his words seem to hang in the air between them.

"Oh." Halle's eyes widened.

Blake felt his temperature rise. He searched her face for some indication that his news was good … or bad. For some reason he felt like he'd just told Halle a secret, and he was nervous about her response. She stood there in silence, so he seamlessly moved to her side, put his hand where it loved to sit, and led her to the door. He didn't feel like mingling and his duty for the night was over.

"Blake." A strong voice called out behind him. *Dammit.* He knew that voice. *So close.*

He stopped and circled around, catching Halle's hand to stop her progression. The touch of her hand was soft, and somehow their fingers managed to tangle. He probably should've dropped her hand as soon as she got the hint to come back, but he didn't. A yearning burned low in his belly for her and he wrestled that feeling as he stared into the eyes of the board president of the North Platte River Bank, Myles Thomas.

"Blake, I'm glad to see you here." Myles glanced down at their hands. It was quick, but Blake caught it.

Just perfect. Myles wasn't exactly known for discretion, and he wouldn't ask questions, he'd just assume. *Time to start using this deal to my advantage.*

"Myles." Blake extended his right hand, glad he'd caught Halle with his left. Myles was a nice guy, but he didn't want to talk about the bank right now, or about Blake's impending decision whether to stay on as the bank president or to work at the ranch.

"Have you thought more about our conversation?"

"I have." Blake nodded. "But, tonight, I promised this beautiful woman my full attention. So, if you don't mind . . ."

Best idea of the year to bring Halle here. This is working out better than I expected after all.

"Hi." Halle let go of Blake's hand and hugged Myles. "So nice to see you. How have you been?"

Blake was suddenly jealous of the man who received a full embrace from Halle so easily. Blake had to stop himself for reaching for her hand when she was back by his side.

"Halle. My dear." Blake watched Myles' face soften. "The family is well. Thank you. How about you? We missed you at Thanksgiving."

Thanksgiving? Halle kept her focus on Myles, giving Blake no clue to her emotions.

"Oh, well, you know how that goes." She studied the ground.

Myles didn't wait long before he asked, "Have you talked to your dad?"

"No, Uncle Myles, I haven't." Halle lifted her head and looked right at the man.

Uncle? Blake's head reeled from the new knowledge. He realized he didn't know Halle extensively, but to not know that Myles Thomas was her *uncle?* Did that mean she really did know everything she'd been saying at these events? *She's been lying to me.* Blake could feel his blood pumping in the side of his neck.

"You two are so stubborn." Myles chortled and shook his head.

Halle shrugged. "Family trait."

"You should mend fences soon. There's some big stuff on the horizon."

"Yeah, well, you know as well as I do that is what started this. I'm happy and the shop is doing great. You should come by and see it. I've done a lot to it since the last time you and Aunt Betty were in."

"We'll do that. Maybe go out to dinner afterward?"

"That sounds like a plan."

They hugged again as Blake stood there gawking. He didn't know how to put into words what just happened. Betrayed? Deceived?

He'd told Halle more about himself than he'd ever shared with someone before. Albeit that didn't amount to a lot of information, but it was still more than others had received. And now come to find out, *he* had no clue who *she* really was.

Halle rotated to face him as Myles nodded his good-byes. There was nothing else to say between them. Blake knew what Myles wanted him to do, and now Myles thought he was dating his niece. What a curious story he was in.

"Shall we?" Halle's lips curved up slightly and her face shone hopefully.

"Yes."

Blake started to put his hand on the small of her back but stopped. It didn't seem right anymore. Irritation at being sideswiped by Halle's identity took over his mind. He had thought Halle was not of his world, that she was innocent in this mess and he was bringing her into it. He'd even started feeling bad that he'd introduced her to this community of people. He didn't have to feel bad now. He had no reason to—she was one of them.

"So, Myles is your uncle?" He tried to sound nonchalant. He didn't succeed. They had managed to make it to his truck before the question exploded from him, and now he sat in his driver's side seat staring at her. He'd started the truck but only because it was a chilly ten degrees outside and freezing to death wouldn't get him any closer to the truth.

"Yep." Halle casually nodded.

Blake's jaw jumped. He wanted her to be more forthcoming. *The woman always wants to talk and now she won't say a word? Typical.*

"And your dad would be ... ?"

"Edward."

I knew it. "Edward Adams," Blake firmly said as he continued to stare at her. Myles's wife and Halle's dad were siblings.

It was dark, but the parking lot light next to them shone into the cab. Her green eyes were surveying him. He could see them narrow at him, too.

"Does that matter?" she asked in a careful tone.

Yes. No. She should've told me. "Why haven't you mentioned this before?"

"Why would I?" Halle's voice started to rise with an edge.

"Why?" his voice raised now, too. "*Why* would you mention that your uncle is on the board—correction—the president of the board, of my family's bank?" Blake shrugged his shoulders, adding to his sarcasm. "The same bank my Grandpa just left to me and I'm supposed to take over?" He tried to put his hand on his hip but, sitting down, that motion didn't quite land. "No need to tell me your father is Edward Adams, either. The man who basically controls all prime real estate and new construction in town. It's not like any of the Ellison businesses do business with him. But, I'm sure you know that. Why do you even need a loan? Why can't you run to *Daddy*?"

Blake watched the rage build in Halle's eyes as he ranted. If he weren't so upset, maybe he would have recognized the need to stop his rant at the beginning.

"My relationship with my dad is *none* of *your* business." Halle's tone was sharp and unyielding. "Why would I tell you *any* of that? We had a deal. You," she shoved her finger toward him, "and me." Halle's finger touched her chest. "Not anyone else. Not my uncle. Not my dad." She shifted in her seat to square up with him. "*You* are the one who didn't want to talk about family and *pressures*, Blake. You don't get to change that now. If it were your business, then *I would have told you*."

The words he'd once used against her stung as she spat them back at him.

"You didn't think mentioning who your dad is with all of his connections to my family was important?"

"No. I didn't. I don't concern myself with his business anymore."

"Why haven't I ever seen you at these things?"

"I have *no* idea." Halle took a deep breath. "You are incredible, you know that? Incredibly self-centered and irritating."

Blake opened his mouth, although he wasn't sure what he was going to say. Thankfully, or not, Halle didn't let him try.

"*Please* take me home." She swiveled in her seat, crossed her arms, and looked straight ahead.

He sat there as well, continuing to study Halle. He was still reeling from all of the information she'd just thrown at him. He pressed two fingers to his left temple in a poor attempt to defuse the beginnings of a headache then jammed his key in the ignition. *Of all the places I could've walked into to get Candace a present.*

He pointed his truck toward her townhouse. He ran through all of the conversations, all of the times she could've said something. She had opportunities. She knew exactly what she was doing with all of that schmoozing. How had he never met her before? He knew her uncle and had met her dad on several occasions, but never remembered seeing Halle. And, from her reaction in her store the first time they'd met, she had no idea who he was either. *I can't believe this.*

There were still three events that she'd signed on to attend: a fundraiser, a feed the homeless charity, and his family Christmas party. *Oh, great.* He wished the last one wasn't less than a week away.

He pulled up to her townhouse. She was out of the truck as soon as he put the gearshift in park. No good-bye. No goodnight. Nothing. Blake watched to make sure she got inside her home safely. He rubbed his hand down his face. If he could just close his eyes and go back a couple of weeks … that wouldn't solve anything.

In all honesty, he thought this night would go a lot differently. He'd pictured, for some dumb reason, that Halle would end up in his arms. That she would put her lips on his and kiss him all over. That was not the case. At this point he didn't know if he still had a date for the rest of the month … or if he wanted one.

Chapter Eight

Halle lit the Christmas lights around her shop, then poured herself a glass of wine. *Stupid men.* She wanted to turn back the tables to the beginning of December and put her closed sign out. *Why did I let myself get wrapped up in all of this? Unbelievable.* Truthfully, maybe not so unbelievable. Halle wasn't great at dating; all of her past relationships told that tale. But her deal with Blake wasn't dating. It was a mutually beneficial agreement. Except now, she wasn't sure she'd get her benefit.

She let out a sigh, grabbed the wine bottle, and headed to her sitting area in the middle of her store. *I wasn't obligated to tell him. He never asked about my family.* Halle curled her legs under her and continued her pity party until Corrine materialized.

"I thought you had a dealio tonight." Corrine said.

Corrine sat down and took a sip from the wine glass Halle had abandoned. She wasn't in the mood to drink. She wasn't in the mood to do anything.

"Yep. Not going."

"Why not?"

"Don't feel like it."

"Halle, what's going on?"

"I wanted a business loan and the bank said no," her words rapidly spilled out.

There was no use keeping details from Corrine any longer. It would probably feel good to tell her, anyway. Halle would take any comfort she could get right now.

"Then Blake came into the store," she continued as she watched the lights on the trees change color. "He needed a date and I needed a loan. I'm not long time friends with him. I just met him that day." She took a deep breath into an aching chest. "So, we've been going to these functions, had a couple more left actually, and everything was going fairly well." She picked at her light pink polished finger nail.

She shouldn't be upset over all of this. She needed to calm down. Maybe she was just sad about the loan.

"We got into a big fight last night. I'm not going to any more events. Which means no loan for me." Halle rested her head on her folded up knees, then faced Corrine.

"Obviously, there is a lot to talk about here. But why in the world do you need a loan?"

"My independence. I want to be on my own. I don't want to be under Dad's umbrella anymore. I want our relationship to be on my terms; ones that I have a say in."

"Independence needs a loan?"

"To buy a store. I don't want to rent from Dad anymore. I bought my own car, home, and this building is the only thing left financially tying me to him. I like Casper and I don't want to move to where Mom is, so this is the only way. If Dad and I are going to have a relationship, it can't be with strings. He doesn't play fair." She picked up her wine glass and traced the top with her finger. "We could go in on a building together ya know; that'd be fun." Halle tried to lighten her voice.

"What was the fight with Blake about?"

Halle scoffed. "My dad of course. He ruins everything."

"First, he doesn't ruin everything. You turned out pretty good."

"Only because I went with mom."

"Second, how in the world did you two fight about your dad? Blake doesn't like him?"

"I don't know if he even knows him. Blake was pissed I didn't tell him all of the names of my family members in town."

The exaggeration felt good. This whole fight was a bunch of nonsense, so why not take it to the next level of crazy?

"That seems weird." Corrine was always one for pointing out the obvious.

"Apparently Uncle Myles is the president of the board of directors at North Platte River Bank. I guess I knew that, but honestly, it slipped my mind. I just think of him as a pharmacist. That news was apparently a personal affront to Blake because he runs the bank, or is going to run the bank." She shook her head. "I get lost. Anyway, then it got really interesting when he found out who my dad was. That's when he kind of went off the deep end. So, I followed. Hence, no more events."

"I see. So you two called off your little arrangement?"

"It was implied."

"How so?"

"We yelled and I stormed off. I doubt he showed up to pick me up tonight anyway. He'd have to be mental to think I'd go with him anymore. We might run into a cousin of mine who knows a guy who knows a guy who knows Blake," Halle mocked.

• • •

Blake's day had been a blur. One big, irritating whirlwind that he had no choice but to be a part of—except he really did have a choice. He hadn't slept well—barely any—since his fight with Halle. One minute he thought he was perfectly justified and then the next he knew where he went wrong. He shouldn't have jumped down her throat about her being less than forthcoming about her family ties in town.

He'd knocked and rang her door bell two nights ago, standing on her porch like an idiot. He'd stood there for at least ten minutes before giving up.

Halle was calling off their deal. No more escorting her to the holiday commitments he had. No more waiting to see what she'd say or wear next. That wasn't what he wanted to happen. *Ah, hell. I don't know what I want anymore.* That was a lie. He could feel wanting and needing Halle down to the very core of his soul. What he didn't know was what to do about those feelings.

"Mr. Ellison? Jerry is on line one." The intercom line cut into his thoughts.

"Thank you." Blake hit the blinking line. "Jerry. Do you have the Adams' application?"

"I do."

"What's the deal with it? Why was it denied? And why can't I get a copy of it?"

Jerry cleared his throat. "That matter has been handled, sir."

"What matter?"

"After I received the loan application, I received a visit from Mr. Adams personally. He implied that if we gave a loan to Ms. Adams, he wouldn't continue banking with us." Jerry's nervous voice came through on the phone. Blake pictured him sweating profusely at his desk.

"Did he give a reason why?"

"No."

"Why wasn't this brought to my attention?" Blake was doing his best not to yell. He knew Jerry had the bank's best interest in mind, but still. That was a pretty big incident to not know about.

"I know how much business your family does with Mr. Adams in many capacities. I didn't want it to become a big deal for you or your family. And, to be honest, Ms. Adams' approval was right on the cusp anyway. It wasn't hard to justify a no."

"If something like this happens again, Jerry, I want to be notified. I take threats to my business seriously. Understand?"

"Yes, sir."

Blake disconnected and leaned back in his chair. Crossing his hands behind his head, he closed his eyes. *Edward plays a little dirty.* Blake knew that family dynamic all too well. He was in the middle of the underhanded part right now.

For the most part, his family played nice. They helped each other and rallied when necessary. But when they disagreed, boy, they disagreed.

Grandpa had kept the peace among the siblings and other relatives who had stake in the various businesses. Since his death, though, things were falling apart. Namely, Blake's already shaky relationship with his father. His father wasn't considering his side of things.

Halle apparently understood more than Blake had given her credit for. She really would have been the person to talk to about his issues. *She would have understood.* He was a good judge of character. He'd been right about Halle, and she wasn't anything like her dad. Maybe that is why he was drawn to her in the first place—he recognized his own plight in her eyes.

I wonder if she knows her dad interfered with her application. Blake doubted it. If she'd known, he would have seen the confrontation on the news. He laughed. Halle wasn't afraid of confrontation and she wasn't afraid to call people on the carpet, when it served her purpose. She picked her battles. She was smart like that.

Dammit. I miss her. Blake opened his eyes. And that was the truth. *How can I miss someone I barely know?*

They'd spent a considerable amount of time together at the events and he'd come to expect her by his side. When she wasn't at the fundraiser, he was absolutely miserable. He kept expecting her to come up beside him with a new drink and whisk him away from a conversation he didn't want to be a part of in the first place. No such luck.

All the questions as to why Halle wasn't there had sucked also. Had she really made friends with that many people this month? He'd held a steady grin and told them she had a prior commitment. Blake left out the part about the other engagement probably involving his face on a dartboard.

He'd really messed it up this time. And he did care about her.

There isn't any going back and changing what I said now. That thought hit him hard. It was done. It was over. He wasn't going to see her again.

Chapter Nine

Halle knew the next event was at the Feed Wyoming center on Third Street. She felt bad for dodging Blake last week, mostly. So they had a fight. People fight. She should have grown a pair and told him to his face that she wasn't going to the next gathering.

Alas, she couldn't muster the courage to tell him face to face, or call him. Truth be told, she didn't know if he'd think their deal was off or not. She couldn't bear to see him mad, hurt, or dressed up with nowhere to go. Sad eyes, or rather any state of Blake's eyes, were her kryptonite. He should have gotten the hint, but who knew when it came to men.

Today, however, she could act the way she wanted to; needed to. She could man up and be an adult to deal with the situation. And she needed to do good for someone else anyway. Her life needed a purpose. Today, that purpose was feeding the homeless.

Halle found a parking spot close by and strode toward the front door, her head held high. She entered, looking for someone in charge to get her started on an assignment amid the activity, when her eyes unwittingly locked with Blake's. Time stood still and the noise receded. She only saw Blake. The man who had been a total ass the other night. Anger flared in her belly and made its way up to her throat. She wasn't there for him. No. She was there because she'd made a commitment to help people.

She diverted her eyes and looked for anyone else she might know to talk with ... anything to not have to talk to him. She wasn't dumb. She knew Blake would be there. She just wasn't ready for the feeling that seeing him in the flesh brought. *He means nothing to me. I need the loan.* She grimaced. *I'm such a loser. I can't believe I'm here.* She thought about making a beeline for the front door and just calling this what it was: stupid.

But in the back of her mind she had to admit she thought that coming today would enforce their original agreement. Even though she had tried hard to think of another way, Halle had no other means or opportunity to get the money. *Maybe I can act like nothing happened, like we didn't fight, and still get the loan.* She strapped on an innocent expression and headed to Blake. If she was going to fake it, she was going to fake it real good.

He had his hands on his hips, still staring at her, when she reached him.

"What?" She shrugged her shoulders. "Just because you're an ass doesn't mean the homeless have to suffer any more than they already do."

Smart and sassy had always won the day before. It would do the trick again.

• • •

Her cinnamon smell calmed his racing heart. He honestly hadn't expected Halle to show up or to see her ever again. *Does this mean we are back on for our arrangement?* The damn business deal. He should have just asked Halle to go with him to the first event as a date and not made it business. *Why do I make everything about business?* That thought scared the crap out of him. Was he more like his father than he thought? He swore under his breath.

Blake pointed to the kitchen doors. "Grab an apron and put your hair in one of the nets."

He may as well keep it business until he knew what her showing up meant. Halle walked past him and found the kitchen.

Blake was lost in the options of his next move to get his perfect outcome when his mom approached him.

"Was that Halle Adams, daughter of *Edward Adams?*"

Oh, great. Who told her? "Nothing gets by you."

At least he wasn't the last to figure out who she was.

"Wonderful. I wanted to invite her to dinner."

Warning bells sounded in Blake's head. *Dinner? No. No. No.* He didn't want his mom interfering with Halle.

"There she is." His mom peered behind him and a sick feeling took over more of his stomach. This was not good.

"Hello again." Halle's tone was polite.

"You can go over there," Blake pointed to the far end of the tables, "and serve the potatoes." *Just walk away, Halle.*

"Nonsense. You'll stay here," his mom counteracted. "We'll serve the drinks and replenish the empties together."

"That sounds great," Halle said, looking straight into his eyes.

Now she's just screwing with me. She came here to make my life miserable. Well played.

"Perfect." His mom couldn't have been more obvious. "I've been meaning to ask you to Christmas Eve dinner tomorrow night. We'd love to have you."

Halle didn't wait a beat before she answered. "I'd love that. Thank you."

"Excellent." His mom looked to Blake, then Halle, and back again. "I'm sure you two have things to discuss. I need to get some spoons for the potatoes . . ." His mom faded into the background like her words.

Blake shook his head and rubbed his hand down his stubbled chin. "What are you doing here, Halle?"

"For starters, you invited me. This was part of the agreement. Remember?"

"I do. I also remember going alone to the fundraiser."

Ha. Don't have an answer to that, do ya? He wanted an answer, though. Did she hate him or was she only mad? Or—the hair rose on the back of his neck—did she ever care?

"I needed a break." Her words weren't as strong as her last ones.

"*That* was not part of our deal."

"I realize that. But, neither was a history lesson about my family." She cleared her throat. "Fine. Our deal is off. But, your mom invited me to Christmas Eve dinner. So…" Halle winked. "See ya there." She walked away from him, finding a spot by the drinks.

• • •

"Halle."

"Hi, Dad. How's Europe?" Halle cursed herself for not looking at the caller ID on her cell phone before answering.

"It's grand."

She rolled her eyes. Of course it was.

"Hopefully someday you can see these magnificent waters."

Someday she'd like to. Sans her father of course. Vacationing with him would be hell, no matter the color of the sand and water.

"Merry Christmas," she said in an effort to switch topics. "I'm glad you called. I need to give my notice. I'll be moving Just Dandy next month." She held her breath and waited.

"To where?"

"I'm not sure yet. If I don't find a place to buy I might build, which would take me longer to move. I should know by the end of December."

"And where are you getting this money?" The calmness in his voice was eerie.

She hated how cool and collected her dad could be. Blake was different. He tried to hide it, she knew, but she could tell when he was mad, irritated, or adoring. She missed him. She rested her hip on the front counter and surveyed her store. How was she going to get all this stuff moved herself?

"I have my ways." She worked to keep her voice just as airy. "It doesn't concern you."

"I should say it does. You're my daughter. What you do in the community concerns me."

Halle paid attention to his tone, trying to hear any indication of how fast this conversation was going to deteriorate.

"Well, it shouldn't. Anyway, I will have the money and be moving in January. You'll be able to rent this space for February."

"You won't find a good price on a building right now. Rates are high, or do you have that taken care of with *your ways* as well?"

Here it comes. Halle braced her cell phone between her ear and shoulder as she reached under the counter for her beads and necklace making kit she kept at the store. She was going to have a lot of frustration to work out this afternoon.

"We've talked about this, Dad. I'm moving out. We'll talk more about this when you get back; go have dinner or something."

She heard shuffling on the other end of the phone and a muffled female voice, Leigh, the new wife speaking. She liked Leigh. Her dad and Leigh hadn't been together long and she only had about fifteen years on Halle, but her dad seemed happier. And that made Halle happy.

"Hello?" *Bad international connection?*

"I'm here." He cleared his throat. "We've been talking, Leigh and I, and we want to give you the building as a Christmas present. You won't have to move."

Halle's head shot up and her cell phone bounced on the floor. She scrambled to pick it up.

"Are you dying?" She tried to find her voice. *Did I hear that correctly? Surely not.*

"No." He hefted a booming laugh. "It's crazy to leave a location you're established in. I know you want your independence and I know you are as bullheaded as me." He paused. "And, I happen to be in a very giving mood."

Thank you, Leigh. Halle made a mental note to get her something very pretty for Christmas.

"So that's it? You're just gonna sign over the building to me free and clear?"

"Yes."

"No strings?"

His pause was longer than she liked. "Yes."

I don't know if I totally believe that. "Thanks, Dad. I'll think about it."

"Very well. Merry Christmas."

Merry Christmas indeed. Halle set her phone on the counter and stared at it. Did her dad just give her a building? For real? Frankly, there was a fifty-fifty shot this was another way to manipulate her life, Leigh's good intentions notwithstanding.

Surely there were down sides to this deal she wasn't seeing yet. Or, maybe, getting married and being on vacation made her hardhearted father almost human.

If she took her dad's offer she wouldn't need the loan. She wouldn't need Blake. *But I want Blake.*

Chapter Ten

Halle slipped on tight black pants and a dark green glittery top. She wanted to sparkle. It was probably going to be the last time she'd see Blake; she wanted to show him what he would miss out on. She took extra time picking the outfit herself and working on her hair—curling it and using a red flower in the back to pin half of it up. Not that it mattered in the grand scheme of things. The big picture didn't care if her hair was done. She'd gotten everything she wanted. She could take her dad up on his offer to give her the building and be perfectly content. Except, emptiness drained any celebration out of her.

Her restless, end of the year feeling was back with a vengeance and it was making her queasy. She gave herself a pep talk as she applied mascara and brown tones of eye shadow to make her green eyes pop. She was attending the party because Blake's mom had invited her. There was nothing weird about her going. And, if she sensed Blake was interested in more, she'd capitalized on the moment. *No backing down.* She vowed to keep her big mouth in check and hope that the holiday spirit would inspire Blake to see her as more than someone he struck up a mutually beneficial deal with.

She felt sick.

• • •

Blake froze with his beer half way to his lips. *Have mercy.* Halle strolled through the foyer dressed to stop a man's heart. Her top shimmered in the twinkling lights from the two large evergreen trees his mom insisted flank the main doors. Her black pants and heels showed off her long legs and curves. *I have to get to those curves.* He put his beer back down by his side and swallowed hard. His breathing slowed. He kept his face neutral toward the man he was talking to, hoping his reaction to seeing Halle wasn't plastered on his face.

When he couldn't get her out of his mind before, it was because she was so different and kept surprising him with her confidence. Now, after he knew the truth about her roots, he couldn't stop thinking about her. Her. Plain and simple. He admired everything about Halle. There wasn't one thing he could name over the other … she was the whole package. He also kept thinking about their kiss. They'd only shared one kiss but it was enough to hook him forever.

Unfortunately, right now, he had no idea where he stood. She'd been nice but rigid at the homeless center. Tonight would hopefully be different. She showed up. That was a good start.

He decided to be proactive. He headed toward her and let the smell of cinnamon and vanilla fill his senses as he stopped in front of her.

"Hello."

"Merry Christmas." Her familiar green eyes warmed his soul.

"Merry Christmas," he returned. "You're going to need a drink."

"More than likely."

He wanted to lead her to the bar. Would she welcome his hand on her lower back as a guide? *Screw it.* He had to find out, and the quickest way to do that was to put his hand there and see what happened.

She didn't turn around and slap him. She didn't cringe from his touch, but she didn't seem to fully embrace it either. Not like she had before. Her body felt tense under his touch. He clenched his jaw. Knowing she was not comfortable with his touch made his throat tighten. Business partners it was. Or were they even that much now?

"Halle."

His mother had found them.

"Hello, Mrs. Ellison."

"Carol. Please."

Blake glared as his mom hugged Halle. He rolled his eyes. His mom always had an agenda. And this one wasn't so hidden. She wanted Blake and Halle together. A great *public relations* couple is how she'd put it last night to him. His family could make anything about business.

"I'm so glad you made it," his mom continued. "Blake, why don't you introduce her around." She waved with no purpose to the room.

Blake gestured to the bartender for a wine for Halle. Then, because why the hell not, he chugged the rest of his beer and signaled for another.

The women chatted pleasantries for a few minutes, but all Blake could do was focus on Halle. She radiated beauty in an otherwise drab setting. His mother turned to leave and Halle sipped her drink.

"How've you been?" Blake asked.

It was a simple question, but he wanted to know. He'd driven by *Just Dandy* too many times to count in the past couple of days but never stopped in. When he'd first met Halle, he didn't know what he was going to do in his business life. Now she'd turned his personal life upside down.

"The shop has been busy. Long hours." She sipped her wine again. "'Tis the season. I have a break now though. For a day or two at least."

"You'll have time to relax and recoup." Blake smiled at her, hoping to see hers in return. "When do you open again?"

"I'm closed until January second." She stared at him. Hard. There seemed to be something she wasn't saying.

She still needs that loan. Everything came together in an instant. *This is why she showed up at the shelter and why she is being so nice now.* Women didn't get over fights that easily. She was probably still pissed at him. Her need for the money was keeping her anger at bay.

"About your loan . . ." he started but was cut off.

"Blake," Her eyes diverted to the crowd and she spoke quietly. "We don't need to talk about that tonight."

He needed to settle a lot of things tonight. He studied her beautiful face. *Something is different.* She looked at him like nothing else mattered in the world.

"Hold on," he said and looked around, finding his dad, mom, and Myles.

He headed toward them, vaguely aware that Halle was following. He slowed his breathing and made sure his voice would be even when he reached them.

"I've made a decision," he announced to the group. The room stopped. "I won't be taking over the bank," he looked at Myles, "but I'd like to consult and still have a presence. The bank means a lot to me, but it's not where I want to be every day. For now." He switched his focus to his dad. "I will be taking over the ranch."

His sister, Candace, sidled up to the group. *Good. She'll back me up.*

"No," his father snipped. "We're selling the ranch. That decision is final."

Candace piped up. "I vote with Blake."

He nodded at her words. "That means we keep it. Candace and I have sixty-six percent together. Majority." He was thankful his grandpa hadn't included his mom in the ownership or this would be a stale mate.

"That ranch isn't profitable, only a burden. You're not thinking right for wanting to spend your time and energy on it. I raised you better than that."

"Actually, it was Grandpa who raised me better than that. He taught me to go after what I want in life. Follow my instincts."

"Your instincts are wrong," his dad spat the words.

"Boys," his mother commanded. "This is a party. Not a business meeting. We'll discuss this later."

"There's nothing left to discuss. The matter is closed." Blake eyed his father and then turned to Myles. "We'll talk Monday about how I can still be active with the bank." And with that, he walked away.

His grandpa would have understood. Maybe eventually they all would.

Halle understands.

• • •

Halle stood in wonderment as Blake announced his intentions to the group and it didn't escape her how his father rebuffed him. *I know that kind of dad. Way to go, baby, stand up for what you want.*

After Blake walked away she wasn't certain what to do. She was sure he wouldn't be in a mood to talk if she followed him. But even so, she shouldn't stay around this group any longer. As she turned to leave, she heard his father declare, "We raised a fool, Carol. He's got no business sense."

Halle felt anger start at her toes and settle behind her ears. *How dare he.* She whipped around and zeroed in on Blake's father. "You, *sir*, aren't paying attention to your son at all. Do you even know him? Don't you understand what he just tried to tell you? Show a little respect for the wonderful man he's become, apparently despite you. He obviously wants to be a part of the bank and other endeavors. But he also needs to figure things out for himself. And if being outside, working hard, is what he needs to do right now, then so be it. That doesn't mean he'll never do something else or come back to the bank." She took a deep breath to slow the tidal wave of words.

She needed to end her rant before she really said something she'd regret, although she was sure that had already happened. *Good thing I have no chance of ever being a part of this family.*

"Shame on you." She spun on her black heels and headed for the door. No dinner for her—she would have to settle for whatever she had in her cupboards, but that was okay. It was worth it.

Halle looked around for Blake but couldn't spot him in the crowd. *He probably left.* She didn't blame him. After that reaction, she understood why he wouldn't stay in the same room. *At least his sister supports him.*

She wanted to see him. She wanted to comfort him. She wanted to let him know everything was going to be okay. The anger that bubbled in her subsided and was replaced with a sad, sinking feeling. *You can be whoever you want to be, Blake. I know you have the strength to stand up for yourself. Stick to your guns.*

She resigned herself to leaving. The void she felt leaving Blake, however, was stronger than ever.

• • •

Blake stood outside in the cold. He needed fresh air after that debacle with his father. *What was I thinking? That my father would support what I wanted?* He huffed. *Fat chance.* The one good thing about tonight was that Halle was there. Maybe he'd still have a chance to tell her how he really felt.

Blake wanted her with him at every event. He wanted her by his side for everything in life. He knew the path he wanted for his life now and it wasn't complete without Halle.

Sometimes he saw a glint in her eye he thought looked like more than friendship or business. Sometimes he swore he saw an attraction—maybe even love. But only sometimes, and it certainly hadn't been there the last couple of times he'd looked into her eyes. *Except tonight.* Tonight had definitely been different.

Just do it. Just go tell her how you feel. If it didn't work out, he could wake up tomorrow knowing for certain and pick up the pieces from there.

He was walking around the corner to the front of the house when he saw Halle coming out the front door. He stopped in his tracks. She was leaving.

There must be a way to win her over. Blake needed time. There had to be a way for them to have forever.

Chapter Eleven

Halle sifted through her mail at the shop. She wasn't open, but she wanted to switch her displays around and pack up Christmas. She had some New Year's decorations to replace them. *Another year, another struggle.* Halle wasn't sure what this year would bring, but like clockwork, her restlessness had subsided and now she was plain tired. *Maybe I should go see the beaches of Europe.* Except if she spent money on a plane ticket, all she'd be doing was the same thing she was doing in her store—trying not to think about Blake Ellison.

A familiar logo stopped her cold. The bank. She had a letter from the bank. She felt her heart rate increase while it was breaking. He hadn't even come by to deliver the news. A signature on a piece of paper would officially end her communication with Blake. Halle clenched the envelope close to her chest. Now any hope that he'd hand deliver the loan approval as an excuse to see her had vanished. *Wishful thinking.*

"What's shakin' good lookin'?" Corrine sauntered to the counter.

I've got to put a bell on that back door or start locking it.

Halle loved talking to Corrine, but right now she wanted to wallow in a pity party for one.

"Anything good?" Corrine peered at the pile of mail, spying the bank name before Halle could hide it. "Did you get the loan?"

"I don't know. More than likely. Blake's a man of his word." She couldn't muster a smile. The loan felt like a consolation prize. And one she didn't even need.

She'd been avoiding *the* talk she knew her friend would want. To talk about Blake, and all that was Blake, would be to admit he was no longer a part of her life.

"I like him." Corrine took the envelope and opened it.

"You do?"

Halle tried not to think of her whirlwind month. She tried not to focus on how Blake had made her feel and how dull life seemed now without him. There was something depressing about knowing they had no more events to attend and no reason to contact one another.

"Yes. Granted, I don't know him well." Corrine paused to scan the letter. "You got the loan by the way."

"Terrific," Halle deadpanned.

"When he came in to apologize, the way he looked at you. That face, my friend, was the expression of a smitten man."

Halle crinkled her nose in disbelief. "No. I doubt that."

"I know love when I see it. Blake loves you. I see it all the time when I'm fitting wedding dresses and tuxes. I can tell the ones who are truly in love. That's why I check out the legal announcements in the paper, to see if I was right."

Halle shook her head in amusement and crossed her arms. "Thank you for trying to make me feel better. That is what you were doing, right?"

"The point is that one of you is going to have to grow a pair and open the lines of communications. Geesh. Do I need to go to the bank, pretend to open an account, and throw a fit so the bank president will come talk to me before you two can have a conversation? Because I'll do it."

She laughed. The thought of Corrine throwing a fit was both hilarious and mortifying. "I sincerely hope you're joking."

"Try me."

Halle waved a hand to settle Corrine down. "Point taken. The good news is that I don't think you'd find him at the bank. He quit on Christmas Eve."

"Then you better call him."

"I'll let you know what I decide to do. I'm not moving buildings by the way. I sort of reached an agreement with Dad about the store." Halle was happy to have a relevant topic to switch to.

She didn't have it in her to joke around about Blake. They'd both received what they'd wanted. The deal had worked out and he clearly didn't love her. If he did, he would've said something by now. The only thing she was left with was a loan she didn't need and an aching heart.

• • •

Blake had spent every minute of the last couple of days outlining duties he would and would not continue at the bank with first Myles and then the managers. He'd also agreed to stay on until his predecessor could be found, provided that didn't take an unreasonable amount of time. That seemed only fair. While he knew he'd made the right decision for his life, it was going to be odd not coming to the bank every day. He never expected to miss it.

The second right decision to end this year on a solid note? Halle. He loved that woman. He'd never been in love before, but he was determined to do it right. He was going to surprise her at Just Dandy.

He knocked on the front door using the neck of a bottle of wine, holding a bouquet of lilies behind him. The closed sign was out, but he'd seen her car in the parking lot. He glimpsed through the front window and saw a figure heading toward him. The door opened and the sides of his lips turned upward.

"Hi," she said breathlessly with a stunned look on her face. She backed up to let him in. "What are you doing here?" Her eyes were locked on his as she swiveled to stay facing him and let the door close.

"Hey, Blake." Corrine called out from the front counter.

"Hey." He didn't take his gaze from Halle.

"I was just leaving. I'll see myself out. See ya later." Corrine slid through the back door.

"Bye." Halle's voice was barely above a whisper and she, too, didn't move a muscle.

"I came to . . ." Shoot, he wasn't ready to just jump right in. He looked down at his hand grasping the wine and remembered the flowers he held in the other. "Bring you these." He swung the bouquet in front of him.

Halle's eyes reluctantly moved off of him to his hand.

"Aah," she sighed and smiled. "Thanks." She took them and found a vase under the counter.

Blake swallowed hard. His pulse raced and he was forgetting everything he wanted to say to her. A paper with a familiar logo caught his attention lying on the counter. *She received the letter.* Blake took a deep breath. How was he supposed to tell her his soul felt at peace with her if Halle didn't need him in her life anymore? *It's a good thing she knows she got the loan already. Now I'll find out if she really wants me for me.* Blake put one hand in his pocket.

"Care for a drink?" He held up the bottle of wine he'd purchased on the way over. It was the same vintage they'd shared the first time they'd met.

"Are you back to day drinking?" Halle laughed and grabbed two wine glasses from under the counter. Blake recognized the glasses from the first time they'd drank together.

"Oh, ya know, pressures," he taunted Halle with the answer he'd given her a month ago as she led the way to the familiar sitting area in the middle of her store.

He sat in the high backed green and pink chair and drank in the sight of Halle as she filled their glasses. She was back in jeans, and a purple shirt peeked out beneath a tan sweater. It felt like he'd spent years without her, not days.

"Those pressures." She tsked, crossed her legs, and shifted to look at him.

She rose her glass in the air, he followed suit to clink hers before they drank.

"How's the store? You get the letter?"

"Yep." She bit her lower lip and let it slide free.

Blake focused on her full lips and lost all train of thought. He gathered every ounce of willpower to get back to the conversation and not swoop Halle into his arms.

"Where do you think you'll move?" he asked.

"I've gotta funny story for ya." She paused then spoke quickly. "I'm staying here."

"What?"

"I had an unexpected call from my Dad and he sort of gave me the building."

"I see. When did you talk with him?" His head began to spin. She didn't need the loan? How long had she not needed the loan?

"We spoke the day before Christmas Eve."

"But you still came to the party." His question was not a question. She didn't need the loan and she'd still come to the last function. A slow smile spread across his face.

He had her. Halle was his. Relief blanketed his body and he relaxed back into the chair. She hadn't come to the party for money, she'd come for him. There was no doubt what he felt for Halle was real. Now, he had to tell her.

• • •

Halle was so excited she didn't know what to do with herself. He'd brought her flowers. Stargazing lilies. Her favorite. *He really paid attention to our conversations.*

She needed him in her life. She loved him. *Why is he here?* Halle didn't dare hope for what she really wanted. He could've just showed up to wish her well with flowers and wine.

Halle checked him out fully as he ate up the space in the chair. She could feel the familiar effects he had on her take over. She shook her head slightly; she needed to get it together and tell him her feelings. But first maybe she should see if he had a reason for showing up today.

"Why are you here?" she asked bluntly.

All of a sudden Blake was out of the chair and his tall frame overshadowed her. He outstretched his hands. She could see only a smile in his eyes. *That is a smile, right?*

"Stand up," he said.

She set her glass down and rose. They were face to face, and his scent made her heart skip a beat. She missed that smell … the smell that created thrills dancing over her skin until she absorbed it, making it difficult to focus on anything else.

He captured her hands in his.

For all of his imperfections and all of his charm, she loved him. Halle looked into his eyes and questioned her own sanity. *How in the world did this happen?*

There was silence as they stood there hand in hand. Halle didn't move—she couldn't. He moved his hands to her shoulders and she relaxed under his touch as he slid them down, taking hold of her hands again.

She was close enough to kiss him. *What is he doing?* Her heart raced as she hoped she knew what he was about to say, what she wanted him to say.

"Halle." He nervously chuckled before looking beyond her and then back. This time his face was soft, his eyes caring. "I'm in love with you."

The words hung in the air as neither moved a muscle. He didn't keep going and Halle didn't know what to say. Was there a *but* coming? He finally continued and she started to breathe again.

"I love everything about you, and I love how you give me the strength to be my own person. I stood up for what I wanted because of you." A grin tugged at his face. "And I heard what you told my father."

Before she could explain herself, Blake went on.

"Thank you. Thank you for believing in me. And I believe in you, too. I get why you didn't tell me about your family, and I'm sorry I got so angry. It really wasn't about who your family members are. It was about the fact that I didn't know much about you, but I had these feelings that were getting really hard to explain to myself. So, I used that as a way to distance myself." He gripped her hands tighter. "And I was absolutely miserable for it."

Halle nodded. She wanted to speak, but her throat felt like it was closing and the area around her eyes started to prickle with the start of tears. *This man loves me, and I love him.* She swallowed hard, trying to temper her emotions.

Blake leaned in and put his lips on hers. She closed her eyes and let the sensation fill her. His warm lips fit perfectly on hers. She deepened his kiss, feeling her need for him take over. Blake pulled away, resting his forehead on hers.

"Halle, I love you." He stood straight up. "Wow, I can't seem to say that enough." His face radiated joy.

Halle's eyes couldn't contain the tears any longer. They freely rolled down her cheeks.

"I love you, too." She placed her hands on his cheeks, brought his face near hers, and kissed him.

He tenderly broke away from her lips. "Dammit."

"What?"

"This is going to make my mom so happy."

Halle laughed and Blake joined her.

"That's okay because it makes me happy, too. As long as we're happy nothing else matters." Halle wrapped her arms around his neck and decided to never let go.

About the Author

Dana Volney lets her imagination roam free in Wyoming where she writes romances and helps local businesses succeed with her marketing consulting company. Surrounding herself with good friends, family, and delicious cups of hot chocolate, she thrives on moments and memories created with loved ones, especially during the holidays. That's when Wyoming's charm really shines. Dana is bold, adventurous, and—by her own admission—good with plants, having kept a coral cactus alive for more than one year.

A Sneak Peek from Crimson Romance
(From *Wildflower Redemption* by Leslie P. García)

Aaron Estes stood at the window, one hand pulling back the drapes to clear his view. Outside, clouds hovered along the horizon, but he doubted it would rain.

Someone from town—Ross something?—had stopped by earlier and offered to do work. The handyman had scoffed at the chance of rain. "Always cloudy," he'd grumbled. "Never rains."

Aaron had shrugged and told the man politely that he didn't need help. And he didn't—at least, not physical help. Spiritual help, maybe, mental health—the kind of health that comes with peace and contentment. The kind of health he'd probably never find again. He closed his eyes and listened for any sound of six-year-old Chloe waking, but heard only silence. Unwelcome memories tried to push in, and he pressed his lids tighter against his face, unwilling to give in again to the pain.

The memories came anyway: the loud, angry words of a marriage shattering. The cheery morning greeting from the one thing he and Stella still shared—a tiny, precious miracle of motion and light.

Chloe's loud kiss and plaintive complaint when her mother tried to leave without kissing Aaron goodbye hovered near the surface. He could still feel Chloe's huge kiss on his cheeks, hear the petulance in her voice when her mother tried to step around them.

"Mommy, you forgot Daddy's kiss." Stella pecked him on the cheek, and Chloe tugged on her mom's blouse.

"Mommy, don't be silly. Mommies kiss daddies on the mouth."

With lips so tight he could feel her anger, Stella stood on tiptoe and touched her mouth to his. Then he watched as Chloe grabbed her mother's hand, delighted that she was playing mom today, not cop. To Chloe, the world was a game, and everyone in it, players.

He closed his eyes, but the burning didn't go away, so he went back to staring blindly outside. There were no daffodils here, as there were in Alabama, but he heard that just miles north spring came in on carpets of bluebonnets and waves of flaming Indian paintbrush. All the locals raved about the Texas wildflowers. They said he should go see them, but he knew he couldn't.

The scene he'd rushed to just over a year ago crowded in: the hysteria, the cop cars with their flashing red and blue lights; the crumpled body of a child, an injured teacher being wheeled toward an ambulance; and an officer who knew Stella pulling him aside. She'd taken a bullet for a kid, the officer told him. Unfaithful, maybe, arrogant often—but nobody doubted Stella Estes's courage.

The tears rolled down his cheeks and he wiped them away with the back of his hand, trying not to remember that there'd been blood on the daffodils the day the world ended.

• • •

Luz Wilkinson tugged on the girth again and nudged Pompom's belly with a knee. "Let it out, girl," she urged. The little pinto sighed heavily and turned around to nose Luz just as the cell phone in her pocket went off. Her horses would have shied at the sudden blast of sound, and the other ponies would have lifted their heads and pricked their ears. Pompom stood there with that complete lack of interest that indicated absolute lack of intelligence.

Frowning over the pony's deficiencies, Luz fished the phone out and hit the button to silence it. She didn't recognize the number. She hoped it wasn't a bill collector, but knew that it probably was.

"Hello?"

"Uh…hi. Is this Eden Acres?"

"Yes." Luz scratched Pompom's ear while she tried to connect a physical image with the deep, masculine voice. She often toyed with visualizing strangers from their phone calls, and almost always was wrong. Silence pricked her into awareness. Perhaps the caller expected someone more enthusiastic, more helpful. Someone who could offer more than one word answers…

"May I help you?" she prodded when he didn't go on.

Another long pause, then came the abrupt questions: "I heard you have therapy horses? And ponies?"

Luz hesitated. Sometimes children from a group foster home came out to ride, and occasionally a counselor who worked with troubled children recommended exposing them to riding. But therapy? She wouldn't go that far.

"We have horses and ponies," she said carefully. "But who told you we have therapy horses?"

"Esmeralda Salinas," the voice said, no longer hesitant.

Luz wrinkled her nose, picturing the elegant redheaded school guidance counselor with her neat suits and perpetual pep. Living in this tiny community, they'd crossed paths several times. They didn't much like each other, but Esmeralda loved horses. That was usually a sterling quality, but this time, Luz's main yardstick for measuring "good folks" didn't hold water, because the counselor struck her as conceited, plastic, and sneaky. Although they avoided each other as much as possible, she boarded the woman's pricey Appaloosa. Undoubtedly Esmeralda would have liked finer stomping grounds for the horse and herself, but no one else boarded horses in this arid, dying community. Very few still owned livestock.

Nevertheless, Luz was surprised that the counselor had referred any male new to town. The director of the children's group home was an elderly woman, and the other referrals were long-time residents, parents in established relationships, but Esmeralda sending a guy her way? He was not single, then, apparently.

"You're Ms. Wilkinson?" Doubt tinged the deep voice. She'd confused the caller. Didn't matter. Confusion was a constant companion these days.

"Yes," she replied. One word again. He could state his business or not. She didn't care.

"Ms. Wilkinson, I need to talk to you about riding lessons for my little girl, Chloe. Or maybe—" Another brief pause, as if he wasn't sure what he wanted. "Maybe even buying a pony. I need advice on what would be best."

He was a client then. She should be happier than she was. She pasted a smile on her face, hoping it would make her voice warmer, more caring. "Great. Advice is what we do best." Quick questions confirmed he knew how to find Eden Acres, and she clicked the phone off and returned it to her pocket. She realized, a little late, that asking the man's name might have been both friendlier and more professional.

"Screw it," she muttered with unusual ire. "Professional never worked for me, anyway. Come on, old lady. Some kid might actually get a pony ride today."

Half an hour later Luz was feeding the menagerie when she heard tires on the gravel drive. She called the motley collection of rescued animals her menagerie, because it took too long to go into the species, circumstances, and problems she dealt with trying to feed and shelter them day to day. Candy, the burro, butted her as she turned away, and the kitten with no name left its feeding dish to run away from some unseen menace, almost tripping her. She wiped her hands on the sides of her jeans and shut the door separating the odd animals from the handful of horses that were both her treasures and bread-earners.

By the time she made it outside, a dark-haired, broad-shouldered man was leaning against an SUV, frowning. He wore long sleeves and a tie, hardly south Texas pony-buying attire. But she wasn't expecting anyone else.

She walked over and held out her hand. "I'm Luz Wilkinson. Welcome to Eden Acres. Are you—?"

"Aaron Estes." He shook her hand briefly, and then cast another look around the premises. Not disapproving, exactly, she thought. It was more a look of disappointment.

"Why don't we go into the office?" she suggested. "It's cooler." And it was well decorated with new paint and shelves of her mother's trophies, recently polished.

They walked into the barn. The half-open stall doors caught his attention. He pointed at one of the horses. "Pretty. Yours?"

"No." She shook her head, and paused to pet the broad blaze of white running down the mare's face. "This is Domatrix. One of my boarders."

"Doma—isn't this Esmeralda's horse?"

"Yes, as a matter of fact." She leaned against the stall door, slanting a glance at him, surprised that Esmeralda had apparently described Domatrix in detail to a man new in town. No wonder Aaron Estes hadn't flinched at the name, even shortened as it seemed to be. Then again…she thought of the tall, regal redhead and the dearth of men in Rose Creek. A man with a daughter likely meant a married man. That would lessen Esmeralda's interest. Wouldn't it? She pushed away from the mare's stall, and he followed the remaining few feet to the office. She waved a hand at the chairs and took her own place behind the small, bare desk.

"So tell me how I can help," she invited.

He looked down for a minute at his hands before looking at her. When he did finally lift his eyes, she could see why Esmeralda had pounced. The man's perfect features and startling green eyes would stop traffic in lots of places, let alone this one-horse, one-eligible-man town.

"My little girl—Chloe—needs a hobby. Something she'll like that's safe."

Luz studied him, perplexed. Somehow the pieces of the big, attractive man across the desk didn't add up. She supposed she was using stereotypes, but he seemed too hesitant and unsure for his own body. Not as if he was uncomfortable in his own skin, maybe, but almost as if he were fearful of something.

She puzzled over the discomfort he seemed to feel, trying to figure out his connection to Esme. He wasn't family; the Rose Creek gossips knew everyone and every relative, no matter how far flung. The counselor had aging parents and a half-brother down in Laredo. A friend? She discarded that. Esmeralda didn't work weekends, and if he were a friend, she would be here. So the relationship had to be professional. Maybe the daughter he'd mentioned was Esmeralda's client?

"'Safe as opposed to bike riding or playing with dolls? Or safe, fun, and a perfect springtime activity—I'm not sure I know what you mean by safe," Luz admitted. "Riding has risks—the same as pretty much everything."

Aaron Estes growled something that sounded profane and hunched forward over the desk, his face tight. "Don't you think I know that?" After a moment, his face muscles eased into smoother lines. His lips twitched, as if they'd known how to smile, but forgotten. "I'm not as weird as I seem. Just a tad nervous and overprotective."

"But you're not in denial," she observed. "That's got to be good." She smiled. "So, tell me about your Chloe."

Pure, absolute love washed across his face. His lips remembered how to smile and he straightened in his chair. "Chloe's my life," he said simply.

Luz returned the smile, but prodded gently for more insight. "How old is she? Does she like horses? Has she ridden before?"

"Six, yes, and no."

Luz blinked, trying to understand the simple, one-word answers. Saw the dimples appear, and then deepen in Aaron Estes' cheeks. She'd always had a weakness for dimples, dammit! Was he one-upping her? "So, is this payback, or do you always keep things so short and simple?"

He actually chuckled. It was a short little rumble of laughter, but a chuckle.

"Payback, definitely. I was nervous enough about calling and you were anything but friendly."

She thought back on her hesitation to answer the phone, how she'd focused on the pinto rather than concentrating on encouraging conversation. He had her pegged, but she didn't care. Wouldn't. She needed customers, but wasn't in the market for relationships of any kind. And professional? She allowed herself a quick mental shrug. She no longer had a profession. She'd been a teacher, and a good one. She'd surrounded herself with kids and poured energy and love into their lives. Then she'd lost it all, including her daughter Lily. Not her daughter, she reminded herself: Brian's daughter, given to her as one more false promise. Now she rescued discarded animals when she could, and was going broke doing it.

So she pounced on something he said. "You were nervous? About asking if we had ponies?" Slight derision might have crept into her words, because he flinched and drew away again.

"Not about ponies." He paused, looking for the right words. "We don't know each other. Esmeralda recommended riding as a form of therapy." He shrugged. "Telling a stranger your kid has problems is hard."

Her cheeks burned with embarrassment. "I owe you an apology—of course it is." She stood up abruptly, annoyed with herself. "Guess it's attack a stranger day—I'm just not sure why. Would you like to look at Rumbles? She would be the pony Chloe would work with first."

"Sure." He got up too, ignoring her apology, and stretched. Outside the office, one of the horses whinnied, and another kicked at the stall. The pungent scents of the stable reminded her it was time to muck stalls—again. Already. Out of the corner of her eyes, she saw his nose wrinkle.

"Do you even like horses?" she asked, curious.

He slanted a glance down at her and shrugged. "Don't know. Haven't been around them. Not really an animal person."

Before Luz could murmur a response, he stopped, turning towards her and holding his hands out in apology. "Not that I don't like them, exactly. I used to travel, and before that—well, I just wasn't raised around them."

"Okay." Luz gave him her own shrug. "So I guess Chloe's mom will be the main go-between here?"

A muscle in his jaw twitched, and the nervous tension he'd shown in the beginning visibly tightened his body. "Chloe's mom," he said through clenched teeth, "is dead."

In the mood for more Crimson Romance?
Check out *Special Angel* by Nancy Loyan
at *CrimsonRomance.com*.